FRED ADAMS JR.

SHERLOCK HOLMES
THE AFFAIR OF THE CHRONIC ARGONAUT

PROSE PRESS

PRO SE PRESS

SHERLOCK HOLMES
THE AFFAIR OF THE CHRONIC ARGONAUT
A Pro Se Productions Publication

All rights reserved under U.S. and International copyright law. This book is licensed only for the private use of the purchaser. May not be copied, scanned, digitally reproduced, or printed for re-sale, may not be uploaded on shareware or free sites, or used in any other manner without the express written permission of the author and/or publisher. Thank you for respecting the hard work of the author.

Written by Fred Adams Jr.
Editing by Dave Brzeski and Ally Fell

Cover by Jeff Hayes
Book Design by Antonino Lo Iacono & Marzia Marina
New Pulp Logo Design by Sean E. Ali
New Pulp Seal Design by Cari Reese

Pro Se Productions, LLC
133 1/2 Broad Street
Batesville, AR, 72501
870-834-4022

editorinchief@prose-press.com
www.prose-press.com

SHERLOCK HOLMES
THE AFFAIR OF THE CHRONIC ARGONAUT
Copyright © 2017 Fred Adams Jr.

CONTENTS

The Adventures Of The Yellow Paper   Pg 1

The Affair Of The Chronic Argonaut   Pg 71

About The Author   Pg 136

THE ADVENTURE OF THE YELLOW PAPER

Any time I spend a quiet afternoon in the company of my friend Sherlock Holmes, I find myself waiting for something to happen to disturb that stillness. When he is working on a problem, I do as little as possible to break his concentration and consequently disrupt his progress. This day, however, Holmes was engaged in recreation, so I had less compunction about breaking the silence.

The late summer sun shone through the curtains of the parlour in our Baker Street lodgings. A group of American magazines had arrived at the newsvendor that morning, and Holmes was pondering a puzzle in one of them. I was trying to make sense of the political cartoons in *Puck*.

"I say, Holmes, you almost have to be an American to understand their humour. I look at some of these cartoons and wonder what the deuce they're all about, let alone why Americans find them funny."

"Satirizing an adversary is a time honoured tradition, Watson," Holmes said around his pipe. "To make one's foe look ridiculous is a powerful weapon, so much so that Augustus Caesar went so far as to issue edicts against anonymous jests and political lampoons. What is in the cartoon?"

"That caricature Uncle Sam in the striped trousers and top hat is standing at an open gateway marked 'the Philippines' and gesturing like a majordomo for men carrying what look like peddler's sacks to enter. One is obviously an Englishman wearing a pith helmet. One is a Dutchman with sabots and a long pipe, and one is a Russian with his long beard, boots and Cossack's hat. What's the point?"

"It seems *Puck's* editors have taken a step beyond lampoon to outright indictment. It reflects a popular sentiment about the evils of imperialism, Watson. The Americans are nowhere near the grasp of the British Empire, but they are reaching."

"Hmmph. And what are you reading so studiously?"

"Not just reading, Watson, engaging; Lucius Lloyd's puzzle column. Here is a conundrum worthy of your intellect: in a dice game at a fair the operator throws three dice. You can wager a coin on any number from one through six. If one die matches your bet, the operator pays your coin back plus one. If two match, you are paid your coin plus two, and if all three match, you are paid your coin plus three. The question is: do the odds favour you or the game's operator?"

"Well, Holmes, common sense would say that if you choose one number of six and three dice are thrown, the odds are three in six, or if you will, one in two that you would win. So, it appears an even chance, but you did say this was a game at a street fair. I doubt the operator would waste his time on such odds."

"Watson, your Victorian pragmatism carries the field once again. You are correct, but your mathematics are skewed." He leaned forward in his chair and spread his hands. Imagine the possible combinations of dice results laid out on a wheel. How many would there be?"

"Well, I don't know offhand, Holmes."

"Two hundred and sixteen, and how many of those would win if you wagered on one number?"

"I'm sure you're about to tell, me," I said.

"Ninety-one. That means you could lose on one hundred and twenty-five. There are your odds, Watson, roughly four to three."

I snorted. "Well, Holmes, I'll bear that in mind the next time I go to a fair, which now sounds like a misnomer."

Holmes laughed out loud. "Excellent pun, Watson. I can always count on your wry sense of humour."

At that moment Mrs. Hudson knocked at the door. "Mr. Holmes, a gentleman to see you." She handed Holmes a card.

"Please send him up, Mrs. Hudson." Holmes studied the card for a moment. "A Mr. William

Bader, Watson, chief of security for Night Star, Ltd."

"The shipping and importing company," I said.

"The same." Holmes relit his pipe, which had gone out during his mathematical lecture. By the time our visitor entered, a cloud of smoke hung over Holmes's head like a halo.

William Bader was a big man, at least six feet three inches. A thick moustache half covered a set of uneven teeth. His broad shoulders strained his suit coat almost as much as his stomach and his silk *foulard* stock seemed to be near strangling him. He looked as uncomfortable in a suit as a man could.

Holmes rose from his chair. "Mr. Bader, I am Sherlock Holmes, and this is my associate Doctor John Watson. Please sit down. Would you like a hassock to raise your foot? I would imagine your gout is rather painful."

Bader blinked. "My gout? How did you know?"

Holmes smiled. "Simple observation; I heard your tread on the stair and noticed that you favoured one foot. The banister creaked at every other step, suggesting a man of your size leaning rather heavily on it. When you entered, I noticed that your clothing is a rather tight fit, suggesting a man accustomed to physical activity relegated to a more passive role and thus gaining weight. The final clue however was your right shoe, which is a size larger than the left and considerably less worn. A simple deduction, really."

"Your reputation is well-founded, Mr. Holmes." Bader sat in a wing chair. "And if you don't mind, I will take that hassock you offered." I carried the

THE ADVENTURE OF THE YELLOW PAPER

footstool over and as he put his foot on it, I said, "I hope you're seeing a physician for proper treatment of that foot rather than relying on one of those patent medicines vendors hawk on the street. They're little more than cherry-flavoured whiskey."

Bader flushed. "Truth be told, Doctor Watson, I haven't had much time for such things lately." He shifted in the chair to prop the foot at its most advantageous angle. "My job has kept me rather busy of late."

"Since the death of Reginald Harper, the chairman of Night Star's Board of Directors, you mean?" Holmes cocked his head at an angle. "The inquest ruled it death by misadventure. He fell off the balcony of his town house, I believe. That poses a grave misfortune for the company on the verge of a major contract to further open trade with China. This is the first time a private company has negotiated directly with the Chinese government, albeit with the compliance of the Foreign Office. The share price took a quite fall too, on the Exchange soon after his death."

"Yes, Mr. Holmes, and to prevent further losses, it is imperative that what I lay before you be kept out of the public eye." He cast a glance in my direction.

"Have no fear. What you say here will be held in the strictest confidence. In that regard speaking to Doctor Watson is the same as speaking to me."

"Very well. In my opinion Scotland Yard took the easy path. I believe that that Reginald Harper may have been murdered by someone trying to halt Night Star's negotiations, although I can't imagine how the devil it was done. My fear is that if indeed Mr. Harper was murdered, that the other three members of the Board of Directors may be in danger as well. I have their authorization to engage you to look into the matter. When it comes to smuggling, theft or piracy, I'm as good as they get, but murder? I'm out of my depth."

"You are suggesting that someone forced Harper over the railing?"

"If that is the case, I can't see how. He was a rough and tumble sort in his youth and good enough with his fists that even at his age he'd have given as good as he got. I've seen him do it with rowdies on the docks."

"What access exists to the balcony?"

"It opens from his study, a pair of French doors. There is no other access."

"These doors were open?"

Bader nodded. "The left one was; the right was closed."

"And Harper was alone?"

"Yes, sir. The servants said he arrived at home around seven o'clock, had his supper at eight then retired to his study. He received no visitors, and when the police arrived, they had to break in the study door because it was locked from the inside."

"And could someone have been concealed in the room before he entered?"

"Not likely; he kept it locked when he was away and only allowed servants to come in while he was in the room. He carried the key with him."

"And was the key on his person when he fell?"

"No, sir, it was turned in the lock in the study

THE ADVENTURE OF THE YELLOW PAPER

door. That's why the police had to break in."

Holmes was silent for a moment. "Was Mr. Harper despondent?"

"If you mean suicidal, no. I saw him that afternoon, and he was as gruff and bully as ever."

I broke in. "Was Mr. Harper a tippler, Mr. Bader?"

Bader shook his head. "He had wine with dinner, but nothing after that we knew of."

"Another question: did any of the servants hear anything unusual?"

"The maid said she thought she heard a shout just before he fell, but that was all."

"There is something more that you're not telling me, Mr. Bader. Apart from the threats, why do you think he may have been murdered?"

Bader tugged at his straining collar. "This was found in Mr. Harper's fist." He reached into his pocket and pulled out a rumpled piece of yellowish paper a little larger than a playing card. He handed it to Holmes.

Holmes reached for his glass and studied it carefully under the magnifying lens. He touched his finger to his tongue then to the paper, which immediately became transparent. "This is rice paper." He carefully smoothed the wrinkled mass and turned it over. It was blank on both sides.

"What significance did the police attach to this paper?"

"None, sir. As a matter of fact after they unfolded it they left it lying on his desk since it was blank."

Holmes rose from his chair. "Mr. Bader, I

should like to see Reginald Harper's residence before the light fails. "You have a carriage below?"

Bader looked ruefully at his foot. "Right again, Mr. Holmes."

"Will you join us, Watson?"

"Of course." I nodded and stood. So much for a quiet afternoon.

***

As the carriage rolled through Marylebone, Holmes puffed at his pipe and gazed at the blue sky of late afternoon. Halfway to Mayfair, he finally spoke. "I understand that Night Star has met with a certain amount of resistance to further opening China to Western trade."

"Yes, Chinese nationals here and abroad have protested vigorously. They see it as a pollution of their culture, westernizing it, if you will."

"I thought the Opium Wars settled that issue once and for all," I said.

"I've learned that in dealing with the Chinese, nothing is ever settled. They are a long-lived and patient people and aren't much for giving up."

"But the diplomats have agreed on terms, and negotiations have been successful to this point."

"Yes, Mr. Holmes, but a handful of diplomats aren't the Chinese people. There's more than enough of them who'd stop at little to prevent the deal from going through. To them, preserving the Chinese way is all but a religion."

The carriage stopped at the door of a handsome brownstone town house. Three stories above the

THE ADVENTURE OF THE YELLOW PAPER

entrance, a balcony with ornate wrought iron rails projected from the building's face.

"That is the balcony?" said Holmes peering upward.

"Yes."

"The stones are pointed shallowly, Watson," Holmes said. "Not much of a hold for climbing."

"No ivy or other vines to use either," I said.

Holmes craned his neck. "And the roof?"

"The police thought of that detail," said Bader. The only way up there is with a very long ladder, and surely someone would have seen it propped against the house. This place is taller than its neighbours, so it's unlikely anyone could have jumped from another roof."

Holmes studied the façade one more time then said, "May we see the study?"

Bader produced a key that opened the heavy oaken door. "The house is empty now. The servants have been dismissed."

We passed through a foyer shrouded in darkness save for the light of a colourful stained glass window at the first landing of the broad staircase. We walked silently over a thick oriental carpet and mounted the stairs behind Bader's painful limp. As we passed through each floor on our way to the fourth, Reginald Harper's wealth became increasingly obvious. The walls of each hallway were hung with paintings and tapestries that would grace any museum. Unlit chandeliers dripped with crystal teardrops, and ceiling murals depicting the revels of the gods testified to the taste and affluence of the owner.

The study lay at the front of the house. The dark door was ajar, its frame splintered by some constable's heavy foot. We stepped inside and Bader threw a switch. Electric lamps glowed in the fixture overhead, bathing the room in a soft radiance. Whereas the art I had seen throughout the rest of the house was distinctly western, the study's décor was purely oriental. Brush drawings hung on the walls, and delicate jade sculpture and lacquered vases adorned shelves and niches.

Holmes crossed to a wall of bookshelves opposite the door and scanned the titles. He took one from the shelf and opened it. "Reginald Harper read Chinese." A question, not a statement.

Bader nodded. "He was fluent in Mandarin, though he always negotiated through an interpreter. He liked the idea that they didn't know that he knew what they were saying."

Holmes knelt before the fireplace. "Was there a fire the night Reginald Harper died?"

"No, it was a warm night."

Holmes wet his forefinger and held it under the flue. "I feel a draft. The damper is open." He reached his hand upward and I heard him tap his knuckles on the metal flap.

That's a tight niche, Mr. Holmes. I don't think even a bird could get through there."

Holmes nodded, rising. "May we see the balcony now, please?"

The balcony was oblong, eight feet by six and ringed with a three foot railing made of scrolled wrought iron. Flagstones made up the surface. I took the railing in both hands and tugged at it,

THE ADVENTURE OF THE YELLOW PAPER

satisfying myself of its attachment.

Holmes peered over the railing and looked down three floors to the pavement below. "Surviving such a fall would be unlikely for any man. And if someone tied a rope to this railing to climb down, he would not be able to take it after him." He looked upward to the peak of the roof. "I think that will do, Mr. Bader."

The carriage brought us back to Baker Street and as it stopped before our residence Holmes said, "May I have the paper that you showed me earlier?"

"Of course." Bader handed Holmes the now flattened sheet.

"I will contact you within a day and let you know what I find."

***

After supper in our rooms, Holmes spread the paper on the dining table and set a lamp beside it for better light. He stared at the paper for quite some time with and without his glass, then he lit his pipe and sat back in the chair. Suddenly he bolted from the chair and crossed the room to the bookshelves. He pulled a large volume from the shelf and spread it open beside the paper.

"What is it, Holmes?"

"Unless I am wrong, Watson, when Reginald Harper crushed this piece of paper in his hand, he destroyed a work of art in the process."

"Art? The paper is blank."

"Look closely, Watson, at the creases in the paper. Many of them are haphazard from being crumpled in Harper's fist, but others are as straight as a ruler and those lines intersect at like angles making the piece two symmetrical halves."

Holmes tapped the book emphatically. "Here, Watson is a similar, if not identical pattern."

The text was in Chinese. The page showed a rectangle with dotted lines and arrows drawn on it. Holmes carefully folded the paper lengthwise then bent one corner experimentally, inward first then outward. Following the creases, Holmes carefully worked at the paper until finally it showed the form of a bird.

"There you have it, Watson."

Holmes handed it to me and I studied the delicate folds. "So, what significance does a paper bird have?"

"Not simply a paper bird, Watson, a double crane. You see the smaller crane at the tail of the larger. This is a fine example of *Zhezhi*, the Chinese art of paper folding. Think, Watson; in Harper's study, did you see any other *Zhezhi* figures?"

"Not that I recall."

"Nor I. Bader's instincts were correct. If Reginald Harper did not practice the art himself, where did he get the crane, and why would he crush so delicate a work of art?"

Holmes turned the paper crane carefully between his thumb and forefinger. "Watson, this paper bird may be the clue that unravels the mystery. What do you know about rice paper?"

"Nothing specific."

"It is made from the pith of the *tetrapanax papyrifer*, a shrub native to China. Among its functions is the wrapping of food, particularly sweets, to allow one to eat a morsel without soiling the fingers. One simply eats the paper as well. Its taste is all but absent, and it dissolves easily."

"You said functions, plural. What are the others?"

"Secrecy, Watson, for one. A message sent on rice paper can be eaten or easily dissolved in water to prevent discovery."

"But this paper has no message; it's blank."

Holmes gave me a piercing look. "I am beginning to think that the crane is the message."

"And what do we do now, Holmes?"

"Now we find a cab and go to Limehouse. There is a certain Oriental gentleman I need to consult."

The cab clattered over the cobblestones as the June sun sank behind us, throwing the streets ahead into violet shadow. "Isn't it dangerous for us, westerners, to be in Limehouse, Holmes, especially at night?"

Holmes laughed. "Popular literature and bigoted rumour paint the place as dangerous and exotic, but it poses no more peril to us than any other poor neighbourhood in London. If I were you, Watson, I should be more concerned for my purse than for my person."

Limehouse was in fact little more than a slum with its tenements and residences jammed cheek by jowl against commercial and industrial properties; factories, sawmills, lead works, coal yards and other businesses catering to the maritime trade. As we passed along Ratcliffe Road into Limehouse, I saw not only many Orientals crowding the pavements but people of every other ethnicity, most of them sailors on shore leave from their ships. "That's odd," I said, pointing to a façade with a sign in German advertising a beer garden. "What is a German beer hall doing in the middle of Chinatown?"

"Shrewd business sense, Watson. There are taverns and inns as well as brothels and even theatres all along this thoroughfare that cater to specific nationalities. A taste of home in a faraway place, I should say."

Holmes was correct. As we moved through the crowded street, I saw evidence of places catering to Spanish, Maltese, German, Italian, Swedish and Greek clientele. As we neared the Basin, the stench of sewage from the streets mixed with the smell of the sea and the smoke from the myriad cooking fires of pavement vendors to make breathing increasingly unpleasant.

Holmes rapped with his stick on the roof of the cab and called to the driver, "Left here."

The side street was narrow but no less crowded. As we went by, the Oriental faces we passed seemed to look through us as if we weren't there, but I knew full well they were taking our measure and deciding whether we were a threat or an opportunity.

Holmes rapped again. "Here."

The cab stopped and we climbed out before a dingy little shop with Chinese characters over its door. Through the grimy glass of its windows, I saw bundles of plants and herbs hanging from hooks in the ceiling and bins of roots, of dried fruit, and of

THE ADVENTURE OF THE YELLOW PAPER

things indescribable.

"We shouldn't be long—Albert, is it?" Holmes said to the cabbie. "You don't mind waiting for us, do you?"

Albert, a big gruff fellow, reached under his seat and pulled out a stout club. "Not at all, sir. Folks know me around here, and they don't bother me more than once. Take your time."

A spring bell rang overhead as we pushed the door inward. The stench of the outside was immediately replaced by an exotic scent as powerful, heavy incense mixed with the earthy smells of plant and animal matter.

The curtains behind the counter parted, and an elderly Chinese man in a soiled white smock entered from a back room. He stood no more than five feet tall, but his erect carriage and the dignity with which he comported himself more than made up for it. His hair was long, white, and as wispy as spiderweb. It flowed down both sides of his face into long whiskers that reached his breastbone.

When he saw Holmes, he smiled, and his face folded into a set of deep seams like the ankle of an old boot. "Mr. Holmes. Welcome."

"Watson, may I present Sun-Yi Cheng." Holmes dipped forward in a respectful bow and Cheng returned the courtesy. "Cheng, this is my associate Doctor John Watson." We exchanged bows, and Cheng stepped around the counter. "What brings you gentlemen to my shop?" He removed his white smock and I saw he was wearing a black vested suit with a green silk four in hand necktie. His only concession to the Far East was a grey queue that hung below his shoulders. At least I thought so until I noticed his thumbs; each ended in a long, green lacquered nail.

"I hope that you can tell me something about this." Holmes held out the paper crane.

The old man's eyebrows dipped inward as he studied the bird. "Unusual. Most *Zhezhi* is executed with more flexible paper. Rice paper is very brittle when it is dry. You see here at the wing's edge where it was begun to split."

"That may because it has been unfolded and refolded," Holmes said. "What can you tell me about the paper itself?"

He held the bird closer to the light. "This paper was not made here." Cheng touched a wing to the tip of his tongue and paused thoughtfully. "The taste says my homeland."

Holmes nodded. "And the figure of the double crane; does it have special significance?"

"In the myths of my people, the crane is a benevolent figure. It is a sign of good luck and longevity, but as with yin and yang, the bird has two sides. For us it is the protector, the night guardian, but it is a nemesis to an intruder."

Holmes said, "Is there a specific religious sect or political group that holds the crane as a totem?"

"Not that I know, Mr. Holmes, but China is a very broad land." He turned the crane in his hand to view it once again from all sides. "This is part of an inquiry, is it not?"

"Yes, and I must take it with me."

"I hate to defile so delicate a work of art, but I could take a bit of the paper, one wing perhaps, and

THE ADVENTURE OF THE YELLOW PAPER

ask among my people as to its origin."

Holmes considered the possibility. "Yes, that could prove most helpful."

Cheng set the crane on the counter upside down, flattening the wings against the surface. He drew his thumbnail over one wing and it came away as if severed by a scalpel. "I will learn what I can."

"Thank you, Cheng. I believe lives are at stake." We exchanged courtesies and left the shop. As we rode away, I said, "Holmes, those thumbnails of Cheng's ..."

"Sharp as razors. Cheng carries no weapons, Watson. He is his own weapon and has lived long in Limehouse as proof of it."

"And his 'people?'"

"Mr. Cheng has his own group of Irregulars among the Chinese youth in Limehouse. If anyone can root out the source of that bird or the rice paper from which it is made, Cheng will."

When the cab arrived at Baker Street, I saw Bader's carriage waiting at the curb and Bader standing beside it.

"Mr. Holmes. I'm glad to have found you. Another member of the Night Star Board is dead."

"What happened?"

"It's Arthur Combs, sir, and from what the police tell me, he's choked to death just an hour ago."

***

Arthur Combs's mansion occupied a corner lot in Knightsbridge. The house towered over trees, gardens and fountains that testified to his prosperity. But the gaiety of the bright flowers was offset by the black hearse that stood in wait under the *porte cochère*. A half dozen uniformed men milled around the front door, and two guarded the gate, keeping out the curious.

Bader's driver spoke to one of the officers at the gate, and the carriage was admitted. As they rolled up the drive, I saw Inspector Lestrade come bustling out of the house. He saw us as well and was beside the carriage before we could disembark. "Holmes, what the devil are you doing here?"

Holmes smiled affably and said. "I was invited by Mr. Bader, Night Star's Chief of Security."

Lestrade turned to Bader. "Very well, Bader, you tell me: what is Holmes doing here?"

"He has been engaged by Night Star to look into the death of Reginald Harper, and now that of Mr. Combs, as well." Bader climbed from the carriage. "And if you'll please step aside, we'll be going into the house."

Holmes stood eye to eye with the inspector. "One death may be an accident, Lestrade, and two perhaps a coincidence, but I would suggest a guard be placed on the remaining members of Night Star's directorship before a third cements a pattern."

"Well, we're a step ahead of you there, Holmes," Lestrade snapped. "We've already put men at the homes of the remaining two, Lucius Burke and Erasmus Willet. Give us a little credit for intelligence, won't you?"

Very little, I thought, but kept the sentiment to myself. The sergeant at the door barred our way, but a wave from Lestrade swept him aside and we entered the mansion. The chandelier overhead reflected in the marble floor of the foyer and from the gilded mirrors that lined the entrance. The servants were lined up along the wall. Some wept and wrung their hands while others maintained the stoic countenance characteristic of the British personality.

Lestrade accompanied us to the library at the rear of the ground floor. A constable stood by the door. The room was lined with bookshelves floor to ceiling on two walls and a third was dominated by open French doors that led onto a terrace and a rose garden. The fourth wall featured a cold fireplace.

Arthur Combs's body was slumped in a leather armchair, his face blue and his tongue lolled out. His collar had been undone and his shirt torn open halfway to his waist, with the placket still clutched in his grip. His eyes were wide and displayed a look of frenzy. A slipper lay on the carpet, its mate on Combs's foot.

A crystal snifter lay on the floor beside the slipper. Holmes carefully picked it up by the edge of its base and put it to his nose. "Brandy." He felt the carpet. "Still damp from the spillage." He turned toward the end of the room. "Those doors were open to the terrace?"

"Yes, Holmes," said Lestrade impatiently. "My men have already searched the grounds and at first light we'll go over it all thoroughly for footprints and other traces of an intruder."

Holmes stood for a full minute staring at the room before he spoke again. "Who found Mr.

Combs?"

"Claymore, the butler," Lestrade replied. He was passing by the open door of the study and heard thrashing. He went in immediately and found Combs in his final throes. He realized that the man was choking and tried to clear his throat, but by the time he did, it was too late."

"What choked him?"

"This." Lestrade took a small bottle from his coat pocket and handed it to Holmes. The bottle held a yellow viscous wad that looked like congealed rice pudding. Holmes plucked the paper crane from his vest and compared it. They were the same shade of yellow.

"What's that?" said Lestrade.

"A piece of evidence you ignored at the Harper town house."

"Where did you get that?"

"I gave it to him," Bader cut in. "You disregarded it and left it at the scene as unimportant."

"It's evidence. Hand it over, Holmes."

"Evidence of what, Lestrade?" I said. "The inquest declared the Harper death an accident and closed the case."

Lestrade's face reddened. "Combs's death puts this all in a different light."

"So now you are investigating both deaths as murders?" Holmes gave him a piercing look.

"Yes. I'm reopening the investigation into Reginald Harper's death. Satisfied, Holmes?"

"Eminently." Holmes handed the paper bird to Lestrade, and as he did, I noted that its tail was

THE ADVENTURE OF THE YELLOW PAPER

missing.

"The paper was crumpled in a ball when we found it. What's this?"

"A paper crane, Lestrade. The creases in the paper suggested the folds. I have a question for Claymore. Would you summon him, please?" Lestrade blinked at the sudden change of tack and spoke to the officer at the entrance. In a moment, Claymore came in.

"Claymore," said Lestrade, "this is Mr. Holmes. He has something to ask you."

Claymore looked every bit the man in mourning. The white-haired butler avoided looking at Combs's corpse, and I thought it might be charitable to cover it. Claymore's eyes were rimmed with red, and the moist dots of tears spotted his pleated shirt front.

Holmes addressed him. "Were the doors to the terrace open all evening?"

"Yes, sir. Since late afternoon to let in cool air from the shady side of the house."

Holmes nodded. "And is this a standard procedure in such weather?"

"Yes, sir, although I did suggest to Himself that I close them because I feared the moths would come in."

"Moths?"

"Yes sir. They get in from the garden from time to time and play havoc with the woollens. I saw some dancing outside, attracted by the light, and I offered to close the doors, but Mr. Combs was enjoying the night air and instructed me to leave them ajar."

"And at what time was this?"

"Just a few moments before—before …" Claymore's chin began to quiver.

"Thank you, Claymore, that will do," said Holmes. The butler bowed slightly and left the room.

Holmes crossed to the fireplace and wet his finger. "The damper is closed. He put an arm up the chimney and felt carefully. "Ah." He withdrew his hand and stood. "Another piece of evidence for you, Lestrade." In his palm, Holmes held a paper butterfly a little larger than a sovereign, blackened with soot. "This was stuck in the flue."

He handed it to Lestrade, who stared at it as if it were the eighth wonder of the world. "Far be it from me to impede an investigation by withholding evidence." He gestured to me. "Come along Watson. There's nothing more to be seen here." Holmes, Bader, and I strode out of the library leaving Lestrade staring open mouthed at the butterfly pinched between his thumb and forefinger as if he feared it might take wing and fly away any second.

Holmes waited until we were in the carriage and on the street before asking me, "What do you make of it, Watson?"

"The gob that Lestrade showed us was sufficient of itself to choke a man, and I suspect there was more that didn't come out. That will be determined at the post mortem, I would think."

"Could it have been regurgitated?"

"It could, but it is unlikely. The wad that Lestrade showed us seemed to be simply dissolved

THE ADVENTURE OF THE YELLOW PAPER

but not digested."

Holmes nodded. "Consistent with rice paper in water, forming a soggy mass."

"So you think someone shoved paper down his throat?" Bader asked.

"I might think so if there were signs of a struggle apart from Combs's death throes. Recall, that Claymore the butler came in as Combs was choking and saw no one else in the room."

"Unless it was Claymore himself who killed Combs," I said.

Holmes turned to Bader. "How likely would that be?"

"Not likely at all, Mr. Holmes. Claymore has been with the Combs household for twenty years or more and has always been a devoted servant. He came after years of service to the late Mrs. Combs's family and remained after her death six months ago. I can't imagine him harbouring any ill will toward Mr. Combs, let alone murdering him."

"Watson," Holmes said, "Did you see food of any kind in Combs's library?"

"Come to think of it, Holmes, I did not."

"Nor did I, Watson. Nor did I. And certainly no Oriental morsels that would explain a rice paper wrapper. It is a puzzle," said Holmes, leaning back in the seat. He lit his pipe and for the remainder of the ride to Baker Street silently contemplated the summer stars.

***

Holmes said little over breakfast, taking long

contemplative pauses between bites of food. I, on the other hand, dug into Mrs. Hudson's excellent breakfast with gusto. When we came home from the Combs house the previous night, Holmes changed into his smoking jacket and immediately picked up his violin. He was still scratching at it when I finally dropped off to sleep. I could see that the puzzle of the Night Star deaths troubled him greatly because it defied logical deduction.

At Holmes's behest, I attended the inquest, which instead of being held at a local public house as was the custom, took place in the operating theatre of Saint Mark's Hospital. The results were a disappointment in that nothing new was revealed. Arthur Combs died as a result of asphyxiation from foreign matter lodged in his throat. In the absence of other physical trauma to his person, the panel ruled Combs's death as a misadventure. Case closed.

I returned to find Holmes shrugging into his Norfolk. "Good that you are back, Watson. A message came from our friend Mr. Cheng. He says he has information for us."

"And we are going to Limehouse?"

"Immediately."

On the cab ride to the East End, I told Holmes the outcome of the inquest.

"I am not surprised. Little evidence, if any, exists beyond the threats against Night Star as a company to suggest foul play. That is, if you discount the other little 'misadventure' that happened to Reginald Harper. Separately, they constitute a pair of inconvenient accidents; together, a convenient coincidence for someone."

THE ADVENTURE OF THE YELLOW PAPER

"But you don't think it a coincidence, do you, Holmes?"

"The odds refute its probability. I agree with Bader that something sinister is afoot; I simply can't see all around it."

"But you shall persist until you do," I said.

Holmes clamped his teeth on the stem of his pipe and disappeared into the labyrinth of his thoughts.

As the cab approached Cheng's shop we saw a crowd on the pavement craning to look through the windows. Two officers stood in the doorway, men I recognized from previous encounters. Holmes shouted over the hubbub of the crowd, "Constable Tate." The officer saw Holmes and none too gently cleared the way for us with his nightstick. "Good afternoon, Mr. Holmes. The Inspector sent for you, I take it?"

Holmes and I shared a glance and neither of us answered one way or the other. "Perhaps you could tell us what you have learned so far."

"Quite a row, sir," said Tate. "Three chinks dead inside. Seems someone tried to rob the wrong shopkeeper."

"Mr. Cheng?" Holmes pressed.

"He's one of the dead, Mr. Holmes, but he took two of the blighters with him."

"Let us see what has happened."

The inside of Cheng's shop was a shambles. Bins were overturned; the roots, plants and herbs were scattered all over the floor. And there was a copious amount of blood. The two assailants lay in congealing pools, their throats cut no doubt by

25

Cheng's razor-edged nails. Cheng lay face down with a dagger plunged to its carved jade handle between his shoulder blades.

"So, one of these men stabbed Cheng, and he killed them both?" I said.

"Don't be hasty, Watson." Holmes pried the eyes of both the dead intruders open, each in his turn. "Look at Cheng's left thumb." The thumb was bloodied all the way to the purlicue as if it had been dipped into a red inkwell. "We're looking for a third man, Watson, a man with one eye. It would appear that Mr. Cheng has taken his other one. As a matter of convenience, I would venture to say that's likely the right eye, the most direct target for a left-handed strike."

Holmes crouched over Cheng's body. "One thing is certainly missing, Watson, his queue."

He raised Cheng's hand. "Here, Watson. Look." Under the hand were scratches in the hardwood floor: a Chinese character. Holmes drew a notebook from his pocket and quickly copied it down. "Let us hope Mr. Cheng didn't die for naught."

"How did he get in here?" A short man in a suit and bowler shoved through the door accompanied by uniformed officers. His eyes blazed behind his rimless spectacles.

"Ah, said Holmes, "Inspector Farraday has joined the party."

"I thought you sent him, Inspector," Tate stammered. "He told me so."

"I did no such thing," Holmes said, straightening to his full height. "Officer Tate asked if you authorized my presence. I did not answer. He inferred tacit acknowledgement from my silence."

"I'll not have you disrupting a murder investigation with your shenanigans."

I noticed that when he stood, Holmes put a foot over the character scratched in the floor. "Do you have no interest in my observations, Inspector?"

"You can take your observations and shove them up your bloody nose." He turned to the officers. "Get him out of here and the other one too."

The Inspector's men advanced and Holmes put his hands up before him. "We'll go quietly. But I would suggest, Farraday, that you might comb the neighbourhood for a one-eyed Chinaman, although I expect he's well hidden by now. Come, Watson; leave these men to their work."

Farraday snorted in derision and turned away, barking orders at his men.

On the street, Holmes opened his notebook to the design Cheng had carved into the floor of the shop. The character consisted of a series of strokes that comprised four parallel downward slashes that fed into a curved line. At the end of each stroke was a dot the thickness of the strokes. To the right the curve turned upward sharply and bent at an angle inward toward the down strokes. A straight stroke projected downward from the middle of the curve.

Holmes caught a Chinese man by the sleeve. "Speak English?" He shook his head. Holmes let him go and accosted another man, a middle-aged fellow in traditional cap and queue. "Speak English?" This time he held up a sovereign and the man nodded eagerly.

"Yes, I speak English good."

Holmes said, "What does this word mean?" and showed him the character from Cheng's floor. The Chinaman's eyes bulged with a look of sheer terror. He tried to wriggle away but Holmes held him fast by his coat sleeve. The man rattled off a string of loud words in Chinese that made the bystanders on the pavement turn toward us. Holmes let go of his sleeve and the man disappeared into the crowd.

The people around us had suddenly lost interest in the show in Cheng's shop and stared at us in stony silence. "I think we should leave, Watson," Holmes said, pocketing the notebook. He raised his hand to a passing cab.

"What do you suppose it means, Holmes?"

"What it means, Watson, is that we have our work cut out for us." As we swung into the compartment of the cab, he called up to the driver, "The British Museum."

"We're going to look for the meaning of that character, I take it?"

"Indeed, Watson. Cheng felt it important enough to leave behind for us with his last breath. It is a match for this." He handed me a ring fashioned from a translucent white stone. Carved in its face was the same symbol we'd seen on the floor. "That came from the finger of one of the assassins. The character's meaning will point us toward the murderers."

"Holmes, you've removed evidence from the scene of a crime."

"There is another just like it on the finger of the other dead assassin. Farraday and his men will no doubt find it." He took the ring from me and studied it carefully. "What do you know about jade, Watson?"

"I saw enough of it in India," I said. "Most of it green. It's a gem, isn't it?"

"No, it is an aggregate, not a crystal, therefore not a gem. The Chinese prize jade and recognize two types as valuable: *Lao-yu*, or green jade and *bai-yu*, white jade such as this ring. The choice of white over green jade for the rings may be symbolic."

"Of what?"

"The Five Virtues: purity, kindness, rectitude, wisdom and bravery. White jade was used to fashion the legendary Imperial Seal, the *He Shi Bi*, or 'Heirloom Seal.' White denotes the divine mandate as purple does in the West."

"And does this mean the assassins believe that they have a divine mandate as well?"

"We are dealing with an extraordinarily dangerous and highly motivated group of people. I hope that translating the word on the ring will give us a clue as to their identity."

Four hours later, we were still seated side by side at one of the long desks under the dome of the British Museum's Reading Room. To one side were piled books that we had consulted and to the other, books we had yet to open in our quest for the mysterious character's meaning.

Holmes and I had methodically turned every page and compared the characters pictured in the massive translation dictionaries with the character Cheng had left us. My eyes ached as did my head, but knowing Holmes, I realized we wouldn't leave until he found what he sought or the Museum closed for the night, and they threw us bodily out the door. I rubbed my temples and with a heavy sigh opened yet another volume, page after page of bewildering calligraphy.

Halfway through the book I remembered that Bader was to come to Baker Street to pick us up at seven o'clock that evening to meet with Lucius Burke and Erasmus Willet. I looked at my watch and realized it would be a close race to arrive on time. I scribbled a note and passed it to Holmes to remind him of the appointment. He nodded resignedly and closed the book he was studying. He stood and motioned for me to follow.

We waited at the foot of the steps watching for a cab. Holmes again studied the *bai-yu* ring as if looking at it long enough would unlock its secret. "A key to solving this riddle lies here, Watson. I'm sure of it."

"Holmes," I said as the cab threaded its way through the busy crowds in the theatre district, "Reginald Harper knew Mandarin Chinese; Burke or Willet might as well. Perhaps they will recognize the character and tell us what it means."

"Some days, Watson, it is the sheer force of your optimism that sustains me."

When we arrived at our lodgings, Bader was waiting, so we were soon on our way to Night Star's headquarters on the docks. The offices were housed in one of the four enormous warehouses Night Star operated in London, bringing goods from every place on earth.

THE ADVENTURE OF THE YELLOW PAPER

"Your employers requested this meeting, correct?" Holmes said.

Bader nodded. "Mr. Burke, actually. He's concerned for their personal safety, of course, but Willet seems to be more worried about the effect the murders—that's what Scotland Yard is calling them now unofficially—will have on the company's posture and the outcome of its negotiations with the Chinese government. Of the two, Mr. Burke seems the most skittish; he wanted to meet in his home and was reluctant to come out of it. It was only when we guaranteed him an armed escort to the offices that he relented."

Holmes opened his notebook. "Watson and I were in Limehouse today. Tell me, have you ever seen this character before?"

Bader frowned. "Not that word exactly, though I have seen many that look similar."

"As have we today for several hours."

Bader squinted at the image. "It could be a new word. Since China opened to the West, their language has had to develop words for any number of things. What is its origin?"

"It was scratched on the floor of a murder scene by the victim. Did you know Sun-Yi Cheng?"

Bader's head jerked up. "The herb dealer? He's dead?"

"Yes, and likely for assisting us on this case. He had information for us, but when we arrived, Cheng was dead. This character was all we could find before the police ordered us away."

"Surely someone knows what it means."

"One person who did raised such a row about it

that we had to leave before he started a riot," I interjected.

Holmes added, "It was as if I had handed the man a scorpion."

Holmes drew a copy of the character on the lower half of the leaf and tore it off. He handed it to Bader. "I understand the intricacy of Chinese calligraphy; a line this way, not that or a dot of ink in the wrong place can change the meaning of a word completely, but this is as accurately as I can render it."

Shortly, we arrived at the Night Star headquarters. Three ships were busily unloading as the carriage pulled up to the gate. Two guards with rifles stood watch. They saluted Bader and opened the heavy wooden gate onto the pier.

"Business seems to be proceeding as usual," I observed.

"You might think so, Doctor Watson, but under the surface, the cauldron is bubbling. I'll let Messrs. Burke and Willet give you their perspective inside. I'm afraid the business side of Night Star lies out of my bailiwick. I can tell you, though, from what I've heard, it's not a rosy picture."

The offices occupied the second floor of the largest of the warehouses. The room to which Bader showed us featured a conference table of polished oak fit to serve dinner to twenty people. The rank of windows facing the Thames gave a panoramic view of the London skyline over the bustling labour on the dock below.

Erasmus Willet sat in a chair to the immediate left of the table's head. Lucius Burke sat to its right.

The head chair stood empty. "Neither of us wants to sit in a dead man's chair, Mr. Holmes." Willet stood. He was a lean man with leonine white hair that flowed into bushy sideburns. An unlit cigar dangled between two of his fingers. I noted a Freemasonry fob dangling from his watch chain. "We sailors are a superstitious lot, eh, Burke?"

"I wouldn't be so cavalier as to joke about it, Willet." Burke was a slight man, a little younger than his counterpart, with a fringe of light brown hair that ringed a bald pate. His mouth was set in a grim line, and his eyes stared through rimless spectacles.

"My colleague is a timid soul," said Willet. "It was his idea, not mine, to meet with you, Mr. Holmes." Willet cast a look at Burke. "He is likely hopeful that you will find a conspiracy sufficient to change my mind. He would like to abandon the China project, but that is impossible." He paused to light his cigar while we waited for the reason. "Such an action requires a majority vote of the Board of Directors, and as of last night, we seem to be one short of a quorum."

"We could appoint a new member," said Burke.

"And you and I could no more agree on whom we might appoint than on the China issue itself. You'd want to appoint someone who'd vote your way, and I'd want someone who'd vote mine." He turned to us and spoke as if Burke were not even in the room. "Burke would throw away a small fortune in expenses and two years of work establishing the China agreement, not to mention millions of pounds of revenue for years to come, all because he's afraid."

"I never favoured this business from the start. It was you and your lodge brothers who outvoted me at every turn." He turned to us. "I've always been the odd man out because I'm not a bloody Freemason."

"What are your objections to the trade agreement?" Holmes asked.

"The risk, Mr. Holmes. Perhaps Willet and his cronies could afford to take a loss, but I don't have their fortunes to gamble. The Chinese are a duplicitous bunch. They can scrape and bow today while they're under the Western heel, but at first chance, I believe they will cut us off and we'll be out millions of pounds. Such a failure would bankrupt the company and ruin me, although my colleagues would hardly feel the pinch."

"Who stands to gain if the negotiations fail?" Holmes said.

"No one, Mr. Holmes," said Willet, "no one. All sides would benefit from a successful expansion of trade. And if we are barred, so will our competitors be, British and otherwise. Trade expansion would benefit the Chinese economy enormously and ours as well."

Bader had moved to the dockside windows and began lowering the blinds. "Oh, for Heaven's sake, Bader," Willet said. "Leave them open."

"I've asked you not to expose yourselves to danger."

"If someone's going to shoot me, and he can't do it through those windows, he'll shoot me while I'm riding down the street in my carriage, or while

THE ADVENTURE OF THE YELLOW PAPER

I'm on the steps of my club, or while I'm sitting in my drawing room. I will not be bullied or cowed by threats. I refuse to live in fear."

"What about Harper and Combs?" said Burke.

"Accidents; unfortunate, but accidents nonetheless."

"Perhaps not, Mr. Willet," said Holmes. "Other factors besides the common business association link the two deaths." He opened his notebook. "Does either of you recognize this character?"

Willet and Burke studied the sketch. "I'm fluent enough in Chinese," said Willet. "But I can't say I've ever seen that one before."

"Nor have I," said Burke, peering over his glasses. "I spent considerable time in China two years ago, and I have some knowledge of the language, but this doesn't look like a traditional Mandarin character. It may be a newly minted word."

"That's what I said," Bader offered. "I've never seen it before either."

"And what connection does this word have with the deaths of Harper and Combs?"

"Of that I am not yet certain," said Holmes. "But I am certain the connection exists. Can the negotiations be postponed?"

Willet snorted. "Are you joking? It's taken two years to get to this point. To halt the process now would derail the whole business and cause irreparable damage to international relations. We are seeing it through, gentlemen, in spite of Burke's misgivings. Our agents in China and the British Foreign Office are in firm agreement."

"If there is an assassination plot, the assassins have spited their own purpose. The death of Combs has made it impossible for us to call a halt by the sheer mechanism of voting. Besides, I have no intention of abandoning the project. I didn't get where I am by being fearful."

"No," said Burke, "You got where you are with the complicity of the Masonic cabal."

"There are no Masons in Peking, Burke." He turned to us again. "If you came here to persuade me to stop the negotiation process, you have wasted your time, Mr. Holmes. But then again, I suppose it is no waste to you since we are paying your fee." He flicked an ash from his cigar onto the floor. "If you have no other concerns …"

"Only for your safety, sir. Confidence is a thin shield at best."

Willet nodded. "That and six bullets." He reached into his coat and drew out a small revolver. "Now if you gentlemen will excuse me, I'm going home." Willet retrieved his bowler from the coat rack by the door and unceremoniously left.

Burke broke the silence that followed. "Let me assure you, Mr. Holmes that Erasmus Willet does not speak for me. I am glad you're here and I am eager for any advice you may have."

"I am sure that if you follow Mr. Bader's instructions, he will be able to protect you. I cannot say the same for Mr. Willet. I appreciate your presence here today, especially under the circumstances. Watson and I will convey our findings to you through him."

Bader sent us back to Baker Street in his

carriage while he remained at the docks. "That fellow Willet is an arrogant one, isn't he, Holmes?"

"Indeed, Watson; it is regrettable, but that kind of man is the maker of the Modern Age, like his American counterparts, Carnegie, Rockefeller, and Frick."

"Hmph. I hope he remembers that pride comes before a fall."

"I should not be so concerned about falling if I were he, Watson. Reginald Harper has suffered that outcome already."

"What are you suggesting, Holmes?"

"That whoever is killing these men has not repeated himself. I believe that if Erasmus Willet is to be murdered, the killer will find unique means."

"And what are we to do in the meantime, Holmes?"

"We shall think, Watson. At the moment that is all that we can do."

The carriage let us off and clattered away. As we climbed the steps to the front door, a voice called from the shadows, "Mr. Holmes."

I turned to see six young Orientals step into the light. My hand slid into my pocket for my pistol. "Steady, Watson. If they meant to do us harm, they would have done it already."

In the light of the streetlamp, the boys looked to range in age from twelve to perhaps eighteen years. Each was dressed in western clothing, several wearing caps or bowlers, but from each, a queue hung behind. The tallest and presumably the eldest approached while the others hung back.

"Mr. Sherlock Holmes?" He removed his hat

and held it by the brim in front of him.

Holmes nodded. "Yes, I am he, and this is my associate Doctor Watson."

The young man bowed respectfully. "My name is Ping Tao," he said in perfect English. My companions and I are the 'sons' of Sun-Yi Cheng."

"Sons?" said Holmes.

"Your word for our station is 'adopted.' All of us were orphans and Master Cheng took us into his care. If it were not for him, we would all be dead or perhaps worse."

"And what may we do for you, Tao?"

"We seek justice for Master Cheng. He was assisting you when he was murdered, and we would hope that you seek the same justice for his killers."

Holmes nodded. "Please come inside." He made a gesture to encompass the entire group. "All of you."

Tao said something in Chinese and the group followed him single file through the door, into the foyer and up the stairs past the wide-eyed Mrs. Hudson.

In our sitting room we hadn't enough chairs for everyone, so Cheng's 'sons' stood in a line that would grace a military drill; left to right, tallest to shortest, oldest to youngest. Rather than taking a seat, Holmes stood as did I out of courtesy.

"Your English is quite good, Tao," I said. "I'd venture to say it's better than half of London's.

"As the first of Master Cheng's sons, I was the first to be educated. My brothers do not speak English as well as I, but they are learning."

"I share in your grief for the loss of Cheng,"

THE ADVENTURE OF THE YELLOW PAPER

said Holmes. "He was a very wise man and helped me on many occasions with his wealth of knowledge."

"He has spoken very highly of you as well, Mr. Holmes. Master Cheng regarded you as an honourable man, one of the few Englishmen he felt worthy of such praise. This is why we come to you. A man who deserves Master Cheng's trust and assistance deserves ours as well."

"What do you have in mind?"

"We respectfully ask that we may be your eyes and ears in Limehouse and the East End, Mr. Holmes. We can go places you cannot, and people who would shun you will speak to us openly."

"You honour Master Cheng with your devotion, and you honour us with your offer."

Tao translated Holmes's statement to his companions. The young men all bowed respectfully.

"We will be at your disposal until this matter is settled, Mr. Holmes."

Holmes briefly outlined the particulars of the case to Tao, who listened in silence, taking in every word and nuance. When Holmes finished, Tao said, "We will begin at once to search for the man with one eye."

"If you do find him, I must ask that you not kill him."

Tao's eyes flashed. "Honour demands it."

"If I am correct, the one-eyed man is a small fish who will lead us to a larger one who has used him merely as an instrument. That man is the true killer."

Tao pondered this thought and said, "We will do

as you wish, Mr. Holmes, for now."

"Where may Watson and I find you tomorrow?"

"I will be at Master Cheng's shop awaiting your instructions."

"One more question before you go." Holmes took out his notebook. "This word was carved in the floor of the shop under Cheng's hand."

Tao looked at the page and took in a sharp breath.

"Doctor Watson and I have not yet been able to learn its meaning."

"With all respect, Mr. Holmes, in Chinese culture every word is a picture, but not every picture is a word." He closed his hand and turned it upward. "It is a picture of a fist."

"And this?" Holmes handed Tao the jade ring.

Tao's eyes widened and he spoke rapidly in Chinese to his brothers. He turned to Holmes. "My apologies for speaking first to them. The ring is worn by members of a secret society in our homeland, The Righteous and Harmonious Fists. We know very little about them, but even here, they are feared by reputation as much as the Tong. This symbol was carved in the floor?"

"Yes. We found it soon after Cheng was murdered."

"When we set the shop to right, we saw no such symbol."

Holmes turned to me. "If someone obliterated it, Watson, I suspect that the other assassin's ring has likewise disappeared."

"If that's the case, Holmes, the conspiracy reaches beyond Limehouse."

"Yes, Watson, and so must we." He turned to Tao. "May we meet in Master Cheng's shop tomorrow at three o'clock?"

"Yes, Mr. Holmes. In the meantime, our search for the man with one eye will begin." At a word from Tao, the young men bowed, turned and filed out of the room and down the stairs.

After they left, I said, "Why three o'clock, Holmes?"

"Because I likely won't find my brother Mycroft in the Diogenes Club before he has eaten lunch."

***

Mycroft Holmes, my friend's older brother, is one of the few people Sherlock Holmes regards as an intellectual equal, and likely the only one he regards as his superior. Mycroft Holmes is employed by the Crown to coordinate information and advise the British government across agency lines. As my friend once said, "At times Mycroft is the British government," influencing policy decisions and guiding the actions of the Empire.

The Diogenes Club, of which Mycroft is a founding member, is a refuge for the unsociable, the recluses among us who want no society yet relish a good chair in a quiet atmosphere where one may read the latest periodicals and enjoy a fine cigar. The atmosphere is beyond the normal quiet of most clubs because one of its strictest rules is silence. No one may speak, upon penalty of expulsion at the third offence.

Holmes sent a note to the club alerting Mycroft to our arrival, and we were ushered into the Strangers' Room, the only chamber in the club where speaking is permitted. To call Mycroft Holmes obese may be medically accurate, but it likely understates the case by half. I long ago abandoned offering my counsel on curbing his weight. On a rainy day, Mycroft would likely weigh as much as his brother and I combined.

Today, as upon other occasions when we have visited him in the club, he was ensconced in a great tan leather armchair, possibly built and provided to accommodate his bulk. Whenever I see Mycroft Holmes, I search his face for the similarity of feature with his brother, and each time, a little more of the resemblance slips away as his features progressively soften. His dark eyes, however, maintain the intensity I've always seen in Sherlock Holmes's eyes, especially when he is discussing a perplexing problem.

"Sherlock, what brings you to see me today?"

"A question you may be able to answer, knowing what you do about the world and all it contains," Holmes said with a grin. "What do you know about The Society of Righteous Fists?"

Mycroft took his time clipping the end of his cigar. He likewise took his time lighting it. "The Society of Righteous Fists is an innocent-sounding moniker for a gang of thugs, rather like the Tong organization that calls itself The Society of Pure Upright Spirits. They are a relatively recent emergence. The Christian missionaries in China have taken to calling them the Boxers because of

THE ADVENTURE OF THE YELLOW PAPER

their fighting skills.

"In the wake of the Opium Wars, the Righteous Fists rose in opposition to Western influence on Chinese culture. To date, they have not been much of a problem, but their numbers and their influence are growing. Has the name come up in connection with the Night Star negotiations?"

Mycroft's leaps of intuition amaze me no less than those deductions Holmes makes on a daily basis. Holmes nodded and said, "I have reason to believe that they are behind the deaths of two principals of the company's board of directors in order to halt negotiations to expand trade with China." He proceeded to tell his brother of events that had transpired to that point.

Mycroft puffed at his cigar and blew a cloud of smoke toward the ceiling. "I am inclined to believe you are correct, Sherlock, given the backlash among the Chinese over their defeat at our hands. The Society of Righteous Fists is using anti-colonial sentiment to recruit new members in the provinces and whip them into a near religious fervour. Their ranks are growing. How much do you know about the Night Star situation from an international perspective?"

"Little more than the papers report. Some factions are beating the drum for them because it will mean an increase in international commerce for the benefit of both countries. Anti-colonialists are inveighing against them, saying that increasing Western commerce in China will diminish its national character and make it simply one more arm of the Empire."

"The Foreign Office and Transport and Trade have been watching the matter closely, and the deaths of Harper and Combs have caused grave concern. The negotiations pose a critical situation in the sense that securing the agreement will give Britain pre-eminence in trade at the expense of the Americans, the Dutch and the Russians. To have Night Star withdraw would cause a great loss of face for the Chinese leaders who have supported this business and damage our relations with China in all arenas for generations."

"But not those of other countries?"

"The general consensus has it that if Night Star fails, all western trade will suffer."

"So, the Americans and others have little to gain by interfering."

"Precisely. The rising waters will lift their boats, and their fortunes, as well as ours."

"The death of Harper and Combs has all but ensured that negotiations will continue, unless, of course, they come to some agreement and appoint a third member to their directorate whose vote could end the process. That seems unlikely as Willet and Burke at loggerheads."

"Perhaps you should simply wait to see which of them is murdered next, leaving the lone survivor in charge."

Holmes stared at him and I stared at them both, then the pair broke out in hearty laughter. "Brother, I can always count on you to put things in their proper perspective. So at this juncture the likeliest culprit is this Righteous Fist Society, with the hope of halting Western influence in their country."

THE ADVENTURE OF THE YELLOW PAPER

"And it is so futile," said Mycroft. "If not this year, the next; if not this generation, then another to come. Change is inevitable and sooner or later the world will become homogeneous despite any sentiment or action to the contrary."

"There is one other matter in which you can be of assistance," Holmes said. "If you would be so kind, I would like you to make enquiries concerning the personal finances of Erasmus Willet and Lucius Burke."

Mycroft nodded. "I shall. You should have the results tomorrow."

Holmes rose. "Thank you, brother."

"Sherlock," said Mycroft, leaning forward in his chair to flick the ash from his cigar, "Look to the paper. Find its source and you will find your killer."

As we left the Diogenes Club the first drops of a cold drizzle fell on my neck. The sky had turned grey since we went inside, and from the looks of the darkening clouds to the east worse weather was coming. "It's a pity we have to go to Limehouse now," I said. This would be an afternoon to build a fire in the hearth and read a good book."

"No doubt many will do so, but there is no rest for us today, my friend," said Holmes. "We have a killer to catch and an empire to save. So, it's back to our rooms and off again."

Holmes was packing a grip when Mrs. Hudson came to the door. "It's Inspector Lestrade and another gentleman to see you and Mr. Holmes."

"Please send them up." I felt flattered. Normally people wanted to see only Holmes. I just happened to be on the premises. "Holmes," I called. "Lestrade is here."

Holmes came out of his bedroom in his waistcoat. "Yes, Watson, and Farraday is with him. I saw them from the window."

The Inspectors strode into the room without a greeting. Holmes picked up his pipe and began filling it. Lestrade looked unhappy, and Farraday looked positively furious. "Holmes, you're withholding information from us, and you're going to tell us what you know about these murders."

Holmes struck a match and made a great show of lighting his pipe. He puffed a moment until his head was wreathed in smoke then turned to Lestrade and said, "Murders? I thought Harper and Combs were 'misadventures.' When did that change?"

Lestrade flushed. "I'll ask the questions, Holmes."

"You'd best start talking, Holmes." Farraday. "What do you know about all this?"

"Inspector Farraday, I didn't think you were interested in anything I had to say. In fact you told me to take my thoughts on Cheng's murder and shove them—"

"I know what I said," snapped Farraday. "But things have changed."

Lestrade cut in. "William Bader is dead."

"Indeed?" said Holmes cocking his head to the side, his only concession to surprise. "When did this happen?"

"That's what we're trying to determine. When was the last time you saw Bader?"

"Watson and I saw him last at the Night Star offices on the docks yesterday. It was late

THE ADVENTURE OF THE YELLOW PAPER

afternoon, perhaps six o'clock, would you say, Watson?"

I nodded affirmation. "Bader sent us back here in his carriage and remained at Night Star."

"Well," said Lestrade, "someone's been at him with a knife; several someones, I should say."

"And where did this happen?"

"In one of Night Star's warehouses. His driver came back to Night Star and was given a note by the gate guard from Bader. The note told him he was through for the evening and to go home. Last night at half two or thereabouts, a watchman on rounds found Bader dead."

"And why has Farraday come with you?"

"Because last evening the street patrol found a gang of Chinese boys on foot in Mayfair. When they wouldn't explain themselves, the assumption was they were up to no good, so the patrol took them to the station. Under questioning, they finally said they had come from a meeting with you, Holmes." He pointed an accusatory finger.

Farraday said, "Lestrade called me in, and I recognized them at once. They're Sun-Yi Cheng's boys."

"And where are they now?"

"In a cell until this is all cleared up," said Lestrade.

"Yes, Inspector. They came here last night to engage me to investigate Sun-Yi Cheng's murder, and I have agreed to do so. Why are you holding them?"

"Because they are Chinese," I said, "and as such, they are immediately suspect when they don't stay in Limehouse where they belong. We can't have them wandering the streets among decent Anglo-Saxons, can we? That is the reasoning, is it not?"

"Don't you get high and mighty with me, Doctor," said Lestrade. I have three murders to solve—"

"Four," Holmes broke in. "Unless Cheng's death doesn't matter because he's not a white man. Wake up, Lestrade. It is all of a piece."

"There is still the matter of what you know about all of this, Holmes."

"I would know more after I have seen the warehouse. Is the scene undisturbed?"

"My men and I have gone over the place."

"Perhaps we could go there now before more damage is done."

Today the gates were guarded by uniformed officers instead of Night Star's men. Lestrade's carriage brought us to Warehouse Three, the furthest from the entrance, where another pair of officers stood watch by the doors. They stepped aside as we approached, and Lestrade led the way into the cavernous building. The warehouse was at least half filled with crates, pallets and bales. Overhead, a spidery network of trusses supported the roof.

Below the trusses a rank of high windows overlooked the water. The light was poor but bright enough that we could see a canvas tarpaulin covering an ominous mound on the floor. Lestrade nodded to one of his men who pulled the tarp away, revealing a ghastly tableau.

THE ADVENTURE OF THE YELLOW PAPER

Bader lay face up in pools of dried blood around his head and his hands. His face was a shredded mass of cuts clotted with congealed blood. His nose and cheeks were flayed to the bone. Tattered ribbons of raw skin and flesh hung from his fingers. The worst were his eyes: the lids sliced away and the eyeballs cut to pieces.

The droplets of blood that dotted the floor around Bader's corpse described a circle of five or more feet. The greatest amount came from his severed jugular and pooled under his head.

"Bader carried a revolver. Was it found here?"

Lestrade nodded to an officer who produced the pistol. "Here it is." Holmes turned it over in his hands and sniffed at the barrel.

"It has been fired recently." He opened the cylinder and checked the cartridges. "All five shots, yet the only blood in the room appears to be his." Holmes walked all around the body, careful to avoid the spatters. "Have you found any of the bullets, yet, Inspector?"

"Yes, one there in a crate on this side of the building, and one in the wall near the doors. We haven't found others as yet."

"You will likely find them embedded in those bales and bolts of cloth." Holmes held the revolver by the handle, in a firing position. He shut his eyes and turned around, pulling the trigger. The hammer clicked on the empty cartridges. "What are you doing, Holmes?"

"Imagining, Watson," he said. "Imagining what a blinded man might do if he were beset from every side. He might spin and fire, and if he were bleeding profusely, especially from his hands, he would throw droplets of blood in a circle as we see here. He still stood before the *coup de grace* was delivered. The droplets fell three to four feet from him, and none appears to be disturbed. Our killers apparently have very long arms." Holmes looked upward into the trusses. "Or they came from overhead."

"Impossible," said Lestrade. They'd have to jump thirty feet, or fly."

"Precisely," said Holmes. He crouched and turned Bader's head to reveal the back of his neck which was slashed as viciously as his face. "Yet in some way, a person or more likely persons surprised Bader, set at him from all sides, and cut him hundreds of times anywhere his flesh was exposed before finally killing him."

"If he fired his pistol five times, why did no one hear it?" I asked.

"Look around you, Watson. The room is piled with bales of cotton and fabric that would absorb the sound. Also, ships are loaded and unloaded here night and day. Any sound short of a cannon firing would likely go unheard outside."

"So, Holmes," said Farraday. "Does this look like the work of the Chinese?"

"Not the lads you are holding, but Chinese, yes. Notice that there are no stab wounds on Bader's body, only slashes. What you see before you is one of the most dire and sadistic punishments of the Chinese culture: *ling chi*, the death of a thousand cuts."

Holmes broke the silence that followed. "Have

THE ADVENTURE OF THE YELLOW PAPER

you been through Bader's pockets?"

"Nothing much to see except this slip of paper." Lestrade handed over a leaf torn from a notebook. I thought for a moment that it was the copy of the fist icon Holmes had given Bader, but when Holmes turned it over, I saw writing on it.

"Lot 137," Holmes read from the paper.

"We've checked with Night Star's shipping and receiving office and found that Lot 137 was a crate filled with artworks." He paused, no doubt for dramatic emphasis. "From China."

"And the recipient?"

"A man named Thomas Beaudry who resides in Mayfair." Lestrade pulled out his notebook. Number 14 Northwest Glendenning Circle."

"And is the crate in this warehouse?" Holmes said.

"It is," said Lestrade. "It is at the rear of the building."

"Then let us see it."

The crate sat in the open at the back of the warehouse. It was a substantial box of planks reinforced with iron strapping. The number 137 was painted on all of its facets, and on its lid was painted Beaudry's name and address.

Holmes walked all around it. "Have you opened the crate?" he said.

"Yes, and it contains what the manifest says it should, statuary and pictures and such." Lestrade gestured to one of his men who pulled aside the lid. Inside were dozens of pieces of porcelain statuary and framed brush drawings heaped carelessly as if discarded by a child.

"Your men seem to have little regard for others' property, Lestrade," I said.

Lestrade bristled. "This is how we found it."

"And nothing was removed?" said Holmes.

"Not a bloody thing. What are you getting at, Holmes?"

"These delicate statues could not have survived an ocean voyage, not to mention handling by the stevedores unless they were cushioned in some way. It is not the art that was of importance. It was the packing material."

Holmes leaned over the crate and peered inside. He moved one statue then another. "Ah." He plucked a shred of yellowish paper from a rough spot in one of the planks. He handed it to Lestrade and said, "Unless I am mistaken, that paper will match the crane you found in Harper's hand. And you have, of course, questioned Mr. Beaudry."

"We would if he existed," Lestrade said with a frown. "Neither he nor the address are real."

Holmes looked again into the rafters then at Lestrade. "You have asked me what I know, Lestrade. I know that the remaining members of Night Star's Board of Directors are in imminent danger from a plot by an anti-colonialist faction called The Society of Righteous Fists that hopes to quash the China trade negotiations." He turned to Farraday. "Is this group known to you?"

Farraday nodded. "I've heard rumours of them, but nothing substantial."

"And how is it that you know this, Holmes?" said Lestrade.

"By asking the young men you have locked up

THE ADVENTURE OF THE YELLOW PAPER

at the Station. I suggest that you release them and allow them to assist me in finding a certain one-eyed Chinaman."

"There you go harping at that damned one-eyed Chinaman again," snapped Farraday. "How do you know he's the culprit?"

"Merely one of them; a simple deduction, Farraday," said Holmes. Then he changed tack, turning to Lestrade. "I hope that you are still guarding Burke and Willet."

Lestrade nodded. "There are men on the grounds of both homes 'round the clock."

"Well then," Holmes said with a mirthless smile, "there is nothing more for us to see or do here. Come, Watson."

We found a cab on the docks and were soon at Baker Street. Mrs. Hudson brought the tea, and retreated, recognizing Holmes's contemplative mood. I did also and withdrew into my newspaper. I had nearly read it through when Holmes said, "Watson, bring a bandage, would you."

I stood and looked across the room to see Holmes standing with a piece of folded paper in his right hand and blood dripping onto the floor from the back of his left. "Holmes, what the devil—"

"An experiment, Watson, and I should say a successful one." He held the folded paper between his finger and thumb. "I have an idea now what killed Bader, and perhaps what killed Harper and Combs as well. All that remains is to find who and how, and the answer may yet lie in that warehouse."

***

Bader's men were back on duty at the gate, members of the Force having left some time earlier. One of the guards, the taller of the two recognized us from our previous visits and opened the gate without hesitation. "Bill Bader was a good man, Mr. Holmes," he said. "He worked us hard, but he was fair, and it ain't right for him to be done for like that."

"We agree," I said.

Holmes eyed the heavy brass ring laden with keys that hung from the guard's belt. "What is your name, sir?"

"Canty, Mr. Holmes," he said. "Alfred Canty."

"If you would, Alfred, please unlock Warehouse Three for us."

Alfred and his partner exchanged a glance then he nodded and said, "Yes, sir. Follow me." As we crossed the dock, Alfred said over his shoulder, "The coppers treated us like dogs, they did, even though it were our boss what got killed. Ordered us about like we was their personal lackeys. That Inspector told us, 'Let no one in the building until you hear otherwise from the Yard.' Well, I figure since you two was with them today, and you come with Bill too before they ever got here, it's all right to let you in. Especially if it helps you catch the blighters what killed him."

The wind had picked up and the water slapped at the pilings of the pier. The cold drizzle that began earlier continued, and fine droplets rolled like crystal beads down the brim of Alfred's cap. The iron keys clanked on the ring as he searched

THE ADVENTURE OF THE YELLOW PAPER

through them for the right one to open the padlock on the warehouse door. "Here we are," he said. In a moment, the door swung open to a cavern of darkness. "Would you like the lamps lit, Mr. Holmes?"

"No, Alfred, I would rather not call attention to our presence, but if you could lend me your lantern, that should suffice."

Alfred handed his small lantern to Holmes and took a larger one from a hook just inside the door for me. "How can I help?"

"If you would, please keep watch outside and tell us immediately if anyone approaches. And if anyone tries to come out of those doors, stop him."

Alfred unslung his rifle from his shoulder. "They won't get past me. I guarantee it."

"Good man," Holmes said. "One more question, Alfred: that catwalk overhead," Holmes played the lantern's beam on the narrow walkway that ringed the building to allow the windows to be opened and closed. "Where is the access?"

"In the far corner to your left." Alfred took the lantern from Holmes and shone the beam at a mound of bales. "Behind them, sir." He handed the lantern back to Holmes. "I'll be just outside if you need me." Alfred slipped out the door, and we were alone in the warehouse.

Holmes stood beside the bloodstains and looked overhead, counting the joists. "We must look above, Watson. There we will find our clue."

A steep stair led us to the catwalk. "What do you suppose, Holmes; that the killer swung down on a rope?"

"That is possible, Watson, but something Lestrade said, that the killers would have to jump thirty feet or fly."

"Neither is possible," I said.

"If the killers were human."

Holmes led the way. The catwalk had a low railing to the inside and the windows to the outside. Across the Thames I could see Big Ben's face and the city lights, a world apart from the odd business we were pursuing. Holmes paced off the distance and counted the trusses. He stopped and shone his lantern below to confirm the location.

"The site of Bader's body is directly below, Watson. Hold the lantern for me a moment, would you?"

He handed me the lantern and climbed onto the railing where he stood full height reaching over his head for the nearest truss. He pulled himself up onto the bottom beam and reached a hand down to me. "Hand that up, would you, Watson."

There was no way for me to do so without climbing onto the railing myself, which I did, but with no small anxiety as I looked down to the warehouse floor. "That's a good fellow," said Holmes. He began weaving his way in and out of the crisscrossing timbers until he reached the centre. He shone the beam of the lantern along the wood.

"There are no marks indicating a rope or chain, Watson," he said. "So your theory of descent seems unlikely. But from here I can see—" Holmes sentence was cut off by a dry flapping sound from the rear end of the warehouse. I turned toward it and almost dropped my lantern at the sight of a bird the size of a man, a bird with angular wings and a long sharp bill, a bird made totally of paper.

The bird flew straight at Holmes who dropped the lantern and twisted himself behind a beam of the truss in time to avoid being knocked from his perch. The bird swooped downward under the truss and flew back at Holmes from the other side. He locked his hands around another beam and swung himself out of its path, but not before one of its wings caught the side of his face and slit it like a razor.

Holmes scrambled toward the catwalk shouting, "Watson, get down!" He leaped from the truss and landed on the catwalk as the paper bird swooped past again. "Shine your lantern in front of me." I heard the rustling wings and swung my lantern to see the bird soaring toward Holmes, its beak aimed for his chest.

With a pirouette worthy of a ballet dancer, Holmes twirled, moving himself out of the monster's path and about again to wrap his arms around it. He then used the momentum of his spin to throw himself through one of the tall windows with a great crash of glass. I rushed to the empty casement in time to see him bob to the surface. Beside him, a flaccid yellow mass floated on the water.

"Holmes, are you all right?"

"Yes, Watson, although I cannot say the same for our friend here."

"Mr. Holmes?" Alfred peered around the corner of the building.

"Alfred. Be a good fellow and throw down a rope, would you."

By the time I climbed down from the catwalk and got outside, Alfred was hauling a dripping Holmes onto the pier.

I shone my lantern onto the river and saw the mass of sodden paper sinking. "I say, Holmes, shouldn't we retrieve that?"

"By the time we reached it Watson, it would be all but dissolved. I did take this, however." He opened his hand and I saw a yellow blob. "I am certain that this will be a match for the mass that strangled Arthur Combs."

In the carriage I was, I must admit, shaken by what had transpired, but Holmes was silent as we passed through the drizzle and mist. Finally I could stand it no longer. "Just what the devil are we dealing with, Holmes?"

"Before I answer your question, Watson, I must ask, are you prepared to challenge your sense of reality?"

"After what I have seen tonight, I have little sense of reality left," I blurted.

Holmes paused thoughtfully before speaking, choosing his words precisely. "I have had my suspicions for some time, and it troubles me to think that they are grounded in truth, but we are dealing with impossibility made manifest, Watson. We are apparently dealing with sorcery."

"Sorcery? Really, Holmes."

"I came here tonight in the hope that the killers would make an attempt on me as they did for Bader. I had to see for myself."

"And you were nearly killed in the process."

"There were neither strings nor wires in the

beams of that warehouse, Watson. The bird that attacked us was no marionette. It was animated by some force beyond our ken, likely imbued in that paper. I am at heart a materialist, Watson, but I cannot refute the evidence of my senses.

"What is established science today would have been regarded as magic three centuries ago, or even more recently. Mundane items you carry in your pockets at this moment would have had you burned at the stake as a warlock in those times. Cause and effect, Watson. Action and result. Those are what we must consider and set our prejudices aside."

"And what are we to do now?"

"Now, we reconsider the facts from a new perspective."

***

We returned to Baker Street soon after to find that in our absence, a large envelope had arrived. It was addressed to Holmes, and its flap was sealed with black wax and a particularly large signet ring I recognized from the hand of Mycroft.

Holmes, still in wet clothes hurried up the stairs and once in our parlour sat in his chair. "Mycroft has been busy, Watson," he said, pulling a sheaf of papers from the envelope. "And apparently what he has found he thinks very urgent."

"At least change your clothing first, Holmes. You'll catch your death."

"I am more interested in catching a killer before someone else catches his."

I dressed the cut on Holmes's face while he

pored over Mycroft's report. He intently read page after page, pausing from time to time to re-read an earlier passage. His brow furrowed with concentration. "It is time to visit Mr. Willet and Mr. Burke, Watson."

Holmes and I climbed into the carriage once again, his only concession to his condition the donning of a dry cloak over his soaking wet suit.

"Do you suppose that either Willet or Burke is the guilty party?" I said as the carriage clattered away.

"Think, Watson. Who would be in a better position to import the paper that is the common denominator of all of the Night Star killings? Either Willet or Burke could easily have arranged for Lot 137 to be delivered to London and would have no problem removing its contents."

"But why would either of them murder the other board members?"

"Control, Watson. One wants the trade agreement, and the other does not. Willet has told us that without a vote against it, the process will continue to fruition. The deaths of Martin and Combs have ensured that outcome. Yet to finalize the agreement requires a majority vote of the board. Burke's death would remove the final obstacle. Willet as the final surviving member could appoint like-minded people to the board and ensure his success.

"If Willet should die, then Burke would be free to appoint board members of his persuasion and the negotiations would cease. The death of either would serve the interests of the survivor."

THE ADVENTURE OF THE YELLOW PAPER

"And why are we going to Willet's house now?"

"I wish to meet his wife."

True to his word, Lestrade had three uniformed guards on duty at Willet's mansion, one at the gate, one at the front door, and one on foot patrolling the grounds. The guard at the gate recognized us, and in a moment we were ringing the doorbell. Willet's butler opened the door quickly and ushered us into Willet's study.

Willet rose from his chair, cigar in one hand and a snifter of brandy in the other. The lights were low in the room, and the fire in the hearth glowed golden in his hair. "Gentlemen," he said. "What brings you here? Good news, I hope."

"We may be very near bringing this matter to a close, Mr. Willet."

"That is good news indeed."

"Is your wife at home, sir?"

Willet blinked. "My wife?"

"Yes, sir. Is she at home?"

"Yes, of course."

"Could you ask her to join us, please?"

Willet looked puzzled but rang for the butler. "Simmons, would you please ask Mrs. Willet to join us?"

The butler bowed his acknowledgement and shortly, the door to the study opened and a stout white haired woman entered. Her blue eyes sparkled in the firelight, and she looked as puzzled as her husband.

"My dear," said Willet, putting an arm around her shoulders. "This is Mr. Holmes and his associate Doctor Watson. I've spoken of them before. They're looking into the deaths of Reginald and Arthur. Gentlemen, this is my wife Jenny."

Mrs. Willet smiled graciously and bobbed her head. "How do you do, gentlemen; how may I help you?"

"How many years have you and Mr. Willet been married, madam?"

"Thirty-two years," said Willet.

"No, Ras," said Jenny with a pat on his arm. "Thirty-three last February."

"Thank you, madam," said Holmes, "and we apologize for the intrusion. Mr. Willet, could you accompany us please?"

"Accompany you where?"

"To Mr. Burke's residence, where I believe we can clear up this matter forthwith."

While Willet was putting on his coat, I whispered to Holmes, "Why are we taking Willet with us to Burke's home?"

"Because, Watson, our recognizance may get us past Lestrade's guards and onto the grounds, but without Willet we may not gain entry."

Burke's mansion stood on a corner lot along Cockspur Street in Charing Cross. It was a three story wooden structure in the current fashion ringed by a spear point iron fence and tastefully polled yews. Like Willet's mansion, Burke's residence was guarded by three uniformed men.

Instead of a butler, Burke himself answered the door still dressed in his business attire. "Willet," he said in surprise. "And Holmes and Watson."

"We would like to speak with you, Mr. Burke," said Holmes. "May we please come in?"

THE ADVENTURE OF THE YELLOW PAPER

Burke hesitated a moment then stepped back from the door. "Yes, pardon my manners. Please come in."

"Where is your butler, Lucius?" said Willet.

"I had to let him go, I'm embarrassed to say, as I have my other servants."

We followed Burke across the foyer into his library where he sat behind his desk and waved an arm to the chairs. "Please, sit down."

"Perhaps we should stand," said Holmes his hand on a ladder-backed chair. My clothing is a little damp. I might spoil the upholstery should I sit." He nodded toward the cold grate. "I would stand by the fire to dry out a bit had you laid one on such a chill night."

"Some of us are less sensitive to the elements than others and can better afford the coal." Burke turned to Willet. "What's this all about?"

Willet nodded toward us. "Ask Mr. Holmes. This visit was his idea."

"Our party is incomplete, Mr. Burke. Would you ask your wife to join us please?"

Burke looked up startled. Willet turned to Holmes and said, "Wife? What wife? Burke is a bachelor."

"To the contrary, Mr. Willet; your partner has been secretly married for more than a year, a marriage he has kept secret to avoid censure. But of course she cannot join us because she is in China, where she was born."

Willet's head swivelled to Burke. "Is this true, Lucius?"

Burke glared at us and did not speak.

"The question of the moment is, Mr. Burke, is your wife being held hostage by the Society of the Righteous Fists to coerce your cooperation, or is your participation in this plot purely for financial gain?"

"This is outrageous," Burke said, anger in his voice. "How dare you come into my home and accuse me of such things?"

"I dare because it is so," Holmes said.

"Sing!" Burke snapped. A tapestry on the wall to our right swept aside revealing a hidden doorway and a man in a mandarin costume, a pistol in his hand pointed at us. A bandage covered his right eye.

"You are too clever for your own good, Mr. Holmes, and I cannot allow you to jeopardize what is being accomplished. My wife is safe and well in the Homeland, thank you. And may I introduce you to Chen Sing, my brother-in-law."

"You've seen to the murders of Harper, Combs, Bader, and Cheng," Holmes said, "for no other reason than to pay off your debts."

"You are wrong, Mr. Holmes. Unlike you, I have lived in China and I have seen the purity, the dignity, the wisdom of its culture, something your Johnny-come-lately British empire would sweep aside like a foolish child at a chess board with its program of westernisation. This is no new sentiment. The Righteous Fists are simply the newest mask of the Brotherhood of the Red Dragon, a society that has laboured covertly to preserve the Chinese way for thousands of years. You were foolish to pursue us to this end, and for your foolishness, you will pay with your lives."

THE ADVENTURE OF THE YELLOW PAPER

"You forget one detail, Burke," Holmes said, resting his hand on the back of the chair. "This."

Holmes spun to his right, taking the chair in his hand and hurling it at Sing. Sing fired his pistol, and I felt the sting as a bullet grazed my ear. A second shot rang out, and Sing crumpled to the floor. Willet had drawn his revolver, which he now aimed at Burke. "You killed my brothers."

"Your Masonic brothers," spat Burke, rising to his feet. "Your pathetic little cabal with its secret handshakes and empty rituals pales before the Red Dragon. You deal in the artifice of men. We deal in the artifice of gods. We deal in magic."

"The magic in the paper," said Holmes.

Burke smiled mirthlessly. "*Zhĭ cikè*, paper assassins; the hand of the Red Dragon reaches across thousands of years to smite our enemies."

***

Pounding came from the front of the house. The officers outside had heard the gunshots and would soon break in the door. The distraction gave Burke the opportunity to pull open a drawer in his desk. I heard a rustling sound that made my hair stand on end. "Your pistol won't save you from these, Willet."

A paper scorpion crawled over the lip of the drawer and dropped to the floor. It scuttled toward Willet and hopped onto his shoe. As it began climbing the outside of his trouser leg, another climbed out of the drawer. Forgetting his pistol, Willet flailed at the paper assailant with both hands.

"Their tails are tipped with poison," Burke said smugly. By the rustling sound from the desk, I realized there were many, many more.

Holmes swatted the scorpion from Willet's leg to the floor where he crushed it underfoot. He reached into his cloak and pulled out a handful of lucifers. He scratched them on the side of the desk then threw the flaring matches into the drawer. The scorpions continued to climb out, but now they were burning as they scattered throughout the room. The drapes went up, and in a moment the library was ablaze.

Burke shrieked with rage and dashed out the secret door. "Watson!" shouted Holmes. "Get Willet out of here." He ran after Burke just before the flames climbed the tapestry. I tried the knob for the other door and found it locked. I heard the constables in the hallway and shouted to them. The door was quickly broken down, and Willet and I barely escaped the burning library alive.

We stood at the gate for some time watching the flames devour the house before a familiar figure appeared from the far side of the place. It was Holmes, his face covered in soot, his hair singed, but very much alive.

"Holmes, are you all right?"

"I am, Watson. My wet clothes saved me. I had to leave my cloak when it began to smoulder. I can tell you, it was a very close thing."

"And Burke?"

"I chased him all the way to a room at the top of the house, the flames right behind us. He had opened a window and was about to climb out of it when the floor gave way beneath him. He is in there, somewhere." Holmes pointed to the inferno. "Now, Watson, let us see to that ear."

Back at our rooms, Holmes treated my wound with more efficiency than gentleness. "How did you know about Burke's wife?"

"Mycroft's report was more comprehensive than simply financial information, Watson. Among the bits of information it included was the unconfirmed rumour that one of the Night Star's board members had a Chinese wife in secret. Combs was a recent widower; Harper was a bachelor but was already dead, and a secret wife would have been no matter. I had only to see Willet's wife and his obvious affection for her to realize that he was no bigamist. That left Burke."

"So Burke was an agent of that Red Dragon Society?"

"An agent, perhaps but not a full-fledged member. He used their sorcery without knowing how it worked the same way most people have no knowledge of the science behind the sulphur and phosphorus of a match when they strike one to light a candle or a cigar."

"Or a paper assassin."

Holmes nodded grimly. "Harper was assailed by a flock of paper cranes, hundreds of them that drove him onto his balcony and over the railing. Then they simply disappeared up the chimney. Combs was strangled by a swarm of paper moths that flew into his mouth and down his throat where his saliva dissolved the rice paper which clogged his airway. Bader was slashed by the sharp edges of the folded paper as dozens of paper birds attacked every exposed bit of his flesh. Their deaths were a practical matter, the methods a symbolic one to satisfy the traditions of the Red Dragon."

"You know Lestrade will be around. What do we tell him?"

"That is something we must very carefully consider, Watson. I believe the whole truth is not for Lestrade's ears, but rather for Mycroft's."

***

The Strangers' Room of the Diogenes Club looked the same as it had on our last visit, and Mycroft Holmes looked as if he had never left his chair. "The Brotherhood of the Red Dragon," he mused. "The Foreign Office knows of the name, but it has always seemed a will o'the wisp. It hides its activities behind whatever faction currently serves its purpose, co-opting the members to pursue its ends. It is unusual that an Occidental would be recruited into its fold, but changing times demand changing standards."

"And what of Night Star and its trade agreement?"

"Its success is all but assured since Willet, as the sole surviving member of the directorate, can make emergency appointments of two new members. I fear, however, that their success will be short-lived."

"How so?"

"The Society of the Righteous Fists grows in numbers daily. Soon they will have sufficient force

THE ADVENTURE OF THE YELLOW PAPER

to mount an insurrection that will undo much of what Night Star has accomplished. Try as they may, though, no one can make progress stand still any more than Canute could halt the waves. China will change from without and from within, perhaps with the slowness of a mountain eroded by raindrops, but it will happen nonetheless."

"Well, brother, I thank you for your assistance."

"It was my pleasure and my duty. You have served the Empire well into the bargain." He thoughtfully stared at the end of his cigar. "And Sherlock," he said, raising his eyes to meet Holmes's gaze. "If I were you, I should tread with care. I fear this business may not yet be over, or perhaps never be over."

***

Nearly a month had passed when an envelope arrived for Holmes. It was postmarked in Wapping two days before. Holmes took his pocketknife from his vest and slit the end of the envelope. He looked inside it and cut it long ways as well. He turned it over and out tumbled a six-inch dragon formed of red paper. The compressed sculpture spread and grew on the table, as if it were coming alive.

"My Lord, Holmes," I said, reaching for my matchbox.

"Steady, Watson." Holmes leaned closer to study the *zhezhi*. This is not rice paper. Judging by its hue and texture, I would venture to say that it is domestic."

"What does it mean, Holmes?"

69

"It means, Watson, that the Red Dragon Brotherhood neither forgives nor forgets. They would like me to know that they are close at hand, and they would like me to ponder my precarious future."

"For God's sake, Holmes, burn the damned thing. We don't know enough about this to be certain what it may and may not do."

Holmes nodded. "Yes, Watson, you may be right." He lifted the dragon by its tail and dropped it into the fireplace.

Perhaps it was simply the crumpling of the paper into ash that made it writhe in the grate, but I felt no bit of draft to help it on its way as it rose from the embers and unceremoniously flew up the chimney.

THE AFFAIR OF THE CHRONIC ARGONAUT

From the journal of John Watson, M.D.:

I set this narrative to paper although it may never see print because I am sure as time passes, and I gradually gain a better understanding of exactly what transpired in November of 1899, I will revisit this manuscript many times and attempt to clarify its content. While I know what has happened and what I have witnessed, the total implications of the events I recount here remain beyond my intellectual grasp. I have changed the names of many of the people who were involved in the business, some for their protection and some for other reasons, but perhaps in the future I will come to understand it all and deliver to you, the reader, a complete and cogent account.

The adventure began as so many do, on November thirteenth with a seemingly unrelated event. I had been lodging with Holmes while my dear wife Mary was in the north attending to a sickly maiden aunt. While I did not see the event in question personally, Mrs. Hudson, our landlady at 221b Baker Street, delivered a vivid first-hand account.

She had just left the house to go to market and had not walked a block up the street when a tall man in a pea coat and cloth cap ran up behind her and yanked her purse from her shoulder. She screamed and caught the attention of a nearby bobby, whose whistle summoned his fellows.

A quick search failed to collar the thief, but Toby Smollet, one of Holmes's Baker Street irregulars, the young lads who assist him from time to time, came running a moment later with Mrs. Hudson's bag in his hand. "A gentleman handed me this, Mum," he said. "Told me he found it in the alley, he did."

"Where is he now, lad?" said the bobby who was first on the scene. "I can't say, sir," the boy told him. "He just said, 'give this to the lady there with the officer. I believe it belongs to her.'"

"My money was gone, sirs," she told us that evening when she brought our tea and recounted the incident. "It wasn't much, just a few pennies, but I must say that being robbed was frightful."

"Nothing else was taken, Mrs. Hudson?" Holmes said.

"No, Mr. Holmes, only my widow's mite."

"And the man who gave young Smollet the bag,

was it the man in the pea coat?"

"Oh, no, Mr. Holmes. The boy said the man was dressed in a walking suit with spats and a derby hat."

"Let us be thankful that you weren't injured by the bounder," I said, and that concluded our discussion of the incident.

As we drank our tea, I commented on the elaborate preparations being made to celebrate New Year's Eve and to welcome in the new century. "Looks as if there will be will be quite an ado outside St. Pauls," I said, looking up from *The Times*.

Holmes grunted. "If people had any sense, they'd realise that centuries run from the start of year one to the end of year double-aught. It's all just an excuse for public drunkenness and revelry."

"You are absolutely correct regarding the advent of the twentieth century, but perhaps the revellers are not so foolish," I countered. "Perhaps they will celebrate this year's end, then admit their mistake and enjoy the second occasion the same way next year."

Holmes snorted and went back to his book.

A few moments later, Mrs. Hudson was tapping at our door again. I opened it and found her holding a small square envelope. "When I went downstairs, I found this showing under the outside door. It's addressed to Mr. Holmes."

I took the envelope from her. Holmes's name was scribed in block letters so neat as to look as if they had been printed on a press. No return address showed in the upper left corner. "Here's a mysterious communication for you."

He studied the envelope and the lettering on its face. "Inexpensive stationery but an expensive pen to draw so fine a line. And very precise penmanship. At first glance the author appears to be a draftsman or perhaps an engineer or architect."

"If he can afford a fine pen, why not fine paper as well?"

"Because good stationery may be easily traced. This may be bought for a penny a quire in most places; common and untraceable. It appears that the source values his anonymity."

Holmes slit the end of the envelope and removed a folded slip of paper from it. He read it and frowned. He handed me the paper and crossed the room to the bookshelves that lined the far wall. I also frowned when I read the message: There is an item of curiosity in Chapman's *Homer*, *The Iliad* Book XXI: 116-117.

"Chapman's *Homer*, eh?" I said. "I recall my school days reading Keats and his poem celebrating it. He compared reading Chapman's *Homer* to Cortez being the first Western explorer to see the Pacific Ocean. Rubbish. It was Balboa, not Cortez, and the lecturer made quite a bit of the fact that Balboa's name better fit the metric scheme to boot."

Holmes already had the volume open on the table. "'Then I felt like some watcher of the skies when a new planet swims into his ken,'" he said flipping through the pages of the book. "Ah."

"So, Holmes, have you found the curiosity?"

"A curiosity indeed, Watson."

"And what do the lines say, Holmes?"

"'Flat fell he on the ground, stretch'd with Death's pangs, and all the Earth imbru'd with timeless blood.' The lines portray the death of Lycaon, but that's not the curiosity. I believe our anonymous correspondent was referring instead to this." Holmes held up an envelope with an address and a stamp. "Here is the curiosity, Watson. The letter is addressed to a Mr. John Jones, *post restante*, GPO North, the new building in Saint Martins-le-Grand. It is postmarked four days ago in Kent."

My brow furrowed. "It would have arrived at the station yesterday. How the devil did it find its way into your copy of Chapman?"

"Perhaps the answer lies in the envelope." Holmes slit the end and drew out another sheet of paper written by the same hand. He laid it flat on the table and I read it over his shoulder. The letter was sealed with a blob of red wax and dated the 9th of November 1899. It read: Garrick Porter will be murdered on the evening of the 11th of November 1899.

"Watson, your paper," barked Holmes. He snatched the *Times* from my hand and spread it on the table, scanning one page after another until he found the article on an inside page: "Gruesome Death in the London Underground." The piece stated that railway worker Garrick Porter, aged thirty-one was found dead along a tunnel excavation of the City and South London Railway. Police furnished little information other than to say that the body had been badly gnawed by the rats that abound in the tunnels, making the cause of death difficult to determine.

"Why would someone send you a letter warning you of a crime that would have already happened?"

"That is the riddle within the riddle, Watson, rather like a nest of Chinese boxes. We lift one and find another inside it." His head raised, and he cocked his ear toward the windows. "Did you hear it, Watson? A carriage has stopped outside." I listened closely and heard a heavy knock at the front door below.

Holmes scooped up the messages and thrust them into the pocket of his smoking jacket. "Not a word of this, Watson. I believe we're about to receive Inspector Lestrade."

Holmes was correct. Mrs. Hudson announced our guest, and Lestrade strode in, a few flakes of early snow lying on his coat collar like dandruff. "Inspector, please come in. Are you here to discuss Garrick Porter?" Lestrade started then his upper lip curled. "You can't fool me, Holmes. You've read the dailies."

"True, but the account in the *Times* had no mention of murder," said Holmes, filling his pipe. "The conclusion is a logical one, Lestrade. Why would you come to visit at this hour if the crime were not a serious one? Further, your clothing brings with it a whiff of formaldehyde and disinfectant." You've been around cadavers this evening."

"Well, I—"

"Further, I suspect you wiped the soles of your shoes when you came indoors, but their uppers testify to a film of grey dust that has since become spotted wet from the snowfall. You've been walking in the tunnel excavation investigating Porter's death."

Lestrade had taken to wearing mutton chops lately and betrayed his sense of agitation by tugging at them with his left hand. By this point in our shared acquaintance Lestrade should have become inured to Holmes's manner; but some reason, perhaps professional jealousy, prevented him from regarding Holmes's deductive ability as a useful tool to be exploited rather than an object of resentment. Lestrade ignored Holmes's amused smile and plunged into the heart of the matter.

"Garrick Porter was found in the early hours yesterday by a watchman on rounds in the tubes. Thus far we haven't determined the exact nature of his death. We turned out his pockets and he still had his watch and his purse with a few quid in it, plus his wedding ring on his finger, so it wasn't a robbery."

"Yet you found signs of a struggle, I take it?" I said.

Lestrade nodded. "Yes, Doctor, the tubes are a grimy place, especially since they've started digging for the new spur to London Bridge; dirt and dust everywhere. We found signs of a scuffle. Porter was a big man, six foot and fourteen stone if he's an ounce, so whoever attacked him must have been a strong fellow."

Holmes said, "The news account said nothing specific about his job. What precisely did he do for the Railway?"

"He was a rat-catcher. There's an irony for you.

He was setting traps when he left the main tunnel and went into a side passage where he was found by the watchman."

"The tunnels abound with derelicts, society's demented outcasts hiding in the dark," said Holmes. "The likeliest situation is that one or more of them killed Porter. I see no great mystery here, Lestrade, except why this perplexes you."

Lestrade turned the brim of his hat in his fingers. "It's something we found at the scene, Holmes, and I don't know quite what to make of it."

"And what might that be?"

"Something better seen than told. If you'll come with me, I'll show it to you."

Holmes turned to me. "Watson, you will join us?"

"Certainly." I must admit, knowing what Lestrade did not about the matter, I was more than curious.

"Then let us go," said Holmes.

***

The weather had turned uncommonly cold the previous few days, and snowflakes swirled in hazy globes around the street lamps. The few pedestrians I saw on the pavements were gloved and scarved, collars turned against the chill. I was glad Lestrade's carriage was a closed one.

We arrived at a large weatherboard building that housed a mining tipple with lifts, cables and chutes to draw the rock and soil from the tunnel below and load it into wagons for removal. Overhead, the giant pulleys were idle. Uniformed officers stood guard around the entrance.

"Where are the workers?" I said. "I understood that the job went on around the clock."

"Sent home," said Lestrade. "I didn't want them in the way and mucking up the scene. Also, I didn't want them taking matters into their own hands and clubbing to death the first tunnel dweller they might find."

"A wise precaution, Lestrade, on both counts."

"And my boys'll see that no one escapes, neither." He nodded emphatically.

Holmes turned his head so that Lestrade couldn't see the amused twitch of his mouth. We both understood that guarding the entry portals made the spidery network of tunnels and passages as secure as a sieve. As we climbed from the carriage, a tall rangy fellow in a long coat and a bowler came out of the building. "That's Clifton Webb. He's a Supervisor for the City and South Railroad. In charge of security, he is. He's not too happy that we're here. Thinks we're intruding on what he sees as a railroad matter."

"But because many railroad police are also civil constables, the official pecking order places them under the authority of the Yard," said Holmes.

"Quite right," said Lestrade, "but that doesn't make him feel any better about it."

Webb began his tirade several paces before he reached us. "Lestrade, how much longer are you going to keep us shut? My employers are breathing down my neck to get the dig working again." Webb's speech was pure West End, dropping Gs from gerunds and ignoring Hs.

"Soon, Webb, soon."

"And who are these blokes?" Webb jerked a thumb at Holmes and myself.

"Those 'blokes' happen to be Sherlock Holmes and his associate Doctor Watson."

"Indeed." Webb cocked his head to the side and squinted at us through one eye. "So it ain't enough you coppers cluttering up the place; you've got to bring in the fancy-pants boys too, eh?" His voice turned to a snarl. "We don't need no 'consulting detectives' nor your interference neither, Lestrade. We can clean our own house. Just let me and my boys down the tunnels and I guarantee there won't be no more bodies when we're done."

Holmes broke in. "Inspector, perhaps Mr. Webb could accompany us and on the way tell us what he knows about the matter and answer any questions I may have." He turned to Webb. "After all, Superintendent, you know these tunnels far better than we."

"Damned straight I do."

"Well then," said Holmes. "Shall we?"

Lestrade and Webb walked ahead of us, arguing like a pair of snapping dogs as we headed into the tipple. I said from the corner of my mouth, "Holmes, why would you tolerate that blustering thug, let alone invite him along?"

"The man is just protecting his territory and his job, Watson. He will be of much more use to us on our side than not, a lesson I wish Lestrade would learn. If I had to choose between the two at this moment, I might well take Webb and leave Lestrade

THE AFFAIR OF THE CHRONIC ARGONAUT

up here."

Inside the building we found a ladder leading down into the tunnel. I had seen pictures of the tunnel work in progress and had ridden the Underground often, so I was not surprised at what I saw before me. The tunnel was circular with a roughly ten-foot diameter, level at its bottom like a flattened hoop. At this stage of excavation, it looked less like a mine than it did an orderly cave. The passage was lit at intervals by oil lamps. "I should think that they'd light the area with electricity," I said, "since the trains run on it now."

"Economy, Watson," said Holmes. The cost to install electric lines as they go and remove them again to finish the tunnel walls would outweigh any benefit. And since there's no danger of gas explosion as you might find in a coal mine, open flames are safe enough. After all, the first underground trains ran on steam."

We followed Lestrade and Webb some distance before I saw Lestrade's adjunct, Sergeant Shepperton with a pair of Bobbies guarding a narrow opening in the tunnel wall. Lestrade pointed. "There is where Garrick was found by the watchman, Holmes, in that passage." Webb handed us lanterns and led the way through the cut.

"Why is this passage here, Mr. Webb?" Holmes said.

"Ventilation. Up ahead there's a vertical shaft to the surface. That's why it's so bloody cold down here."

"Yes, otherwise the temperature would be a uniform fifty-two degrees Fahrenheit as it is in most caves."

Webb turned and eyed Holmes for a moment then nodded and said, "Right you are."

"Tell me, Mr. Webb, how long did Porter work for the City and South?"

"I can't say offhand. He was working when I started twelve years ago."

"And did he ever complain of any disagreements with others?"

"Not so much, although last week he was grumbling to Casey the foreman that he thought someone was opening his traps as a joke. I've seen him take a dozen or more rats out in a single shift. You see, he's paid by the head as it were."

We followed Lestrade through the rough-hewn passage a dozen yards or so before he said, "Here's the place."

"Not much to see," I said. The tunnel was no wider here, and its grey rock walls no different. Two or three yards beyond a disturbed patch in the dust of the floor, a wide drainage ditch gurgled with water. A few flakes of snow fell down the ventilation shaft from above it and disappeared into the turgid stream. Beyond the ditch, the tunnel dead-ended into a rock wall. A few small wooden traps and an empty burlap bag lay to one side.

"On the contrary, Watson, there is very much to see." Holmes crouched to study the marks and impressions in the dust. "I see the prints of several shoes. How many men have been here beside yourselves?"

"Two or three of my men," said Webb. "Theirs are the prints that ain't flat."

THE AFFAIR OF THE CHRONIC ARGONAUT

Lestrade ignored the jibe. He pointed to a print with his toe. "This track matches the shoes Porter had on; see the star in the heel?"

Holmes grunted. "The trademark of T. Martin, a common brand of work oxford. I'm surprised there aren't more of them in different sizes." He turned to Webb. "When the watchman found Porter's body, did he notice anything out of the ordinary in the tunnel?"

"He took one look at the body and run out like the Devil was on his collar," said Webb, "and he raised such a cry that the rest of the workers run right behind him. You see, Mr. Holmes, the men have been a bit skittish lately what with talk of a ghost in the tunnels."

"A ghost?"

"It's bloody foolishness that sprung up a few weeks ago when the diggers working cut and cover found some old bones. 'We're disturbing the dead. There'll be retribution,' says one, and the next thing you know, they're all on it. One says he hears voices, another footfalls, and another the wail of a banshee." He shook his head in disgust. "It weren't no ghost done for Porter."

Holmes straightened up and brushed dust from his palms. "I agree, Mr. Webb. This was the work of very material hands." He turned to Lestrade. "Inspector, what is it that you wanted to show me?"

I saw Webb shoot Lestrade a look and realised that whatever it was, Webb knew nothing about it.

"There, Holmes." He gestured with the lantern. A foot short of the ditch. I kept my men away when I saw the prints. You go ahead; there's not room for two."

"What? What did you find, Lestrade? I want to see it."

"You'll have your turn, Webb," Lestrade growled. "Get back."

Holmes slipped past Lestrade and crouched at the edge of the ditch. "You did well to protect these, Lestrade. Watson, come here and have a look."

I peered over Holmes's shoulder and saw in the dust the prints of a pair of bare human feet about three feet apart and aimed toward the ditch. They were no bigger than the track of a child of ten or twelve years.

"These are the only prints of this type you have found?" Holmes asked.

"Only those two."

"What do you see, Watson?"

"The toes are splayed suggesting a person who has gone shoeless for a long time."

"Very good. What else?"

"As a matter of scale, I think the stride is too long for a pair of legs that match such small feet."

"Unless?"

"Unless he was running. But running to where?"

Holmes eyes turned upward. "He was running for momentum to spring." He angled the lantern to look up the airshaft. "Rough stone, plenty of handholds for climbing."

"So, Holmes, the question becomes who that size could leap that high? It's a good seven feet up."

"Or what, Watson?" Holmes said, fixing me with his stare. "Or what?" He turned to Lestrade. "I've seen as much here as I may for the moment.

May we go now and examine the body?"

***

I knew better than to question Holmes in front of Lestrade and Shepperton, but his last remark opened a wide door of speculation. Holmes lit his pipe and was silent the entire ride to Saint Mark's Hospital where Lestrade had Porter's body taken to avoid the reporters who circle Scotland Yard like a flock of vultures.

Lestrade rapped on the carriage roof and called to the driver to pull to the rear of the building. We stepped out at a dimly lit double door for ambulance delivery. Lestrade pulled the bell.

Shortly a round red face appeared in the doorway. "Evening, Inspector." He chuckled. "That's twice in one evening. People will talk."

"Shut it, Hennessey." He shouldered through the door and motioned for Holmes and myself to follow him. Shepperton brought up the rear.

Hennessey was a stout little man with a fringe of greying hair like a horseshoe above his ears. Dressed in a shop apron, he would look the part of a neighbourhood butcher. Dressed in a bloody laboratory smock, his jovial manner seemed jarringly inappropriate. He rattled on as he led the way through the hospital basement. "Right this way, sirs. Is it the same guest you'll be visiting, Inspector?"

"Porter."

"He's a popular one, that Porter is," Hennessey said. "First you come in to see him, then you send that other policeman, and now you bring these two gents—"

"What other policeman?"

Hennessey scratched his head in a pantomime of thought. "Baines? Barnes? Barrett. That was the name on his credentials."

"I sent no such person, Hennessey. I—"

Holmes cut in. "What was the appearance of this Barrett fellow?"

"A bit tall, sir; of course to me everyone seems a bit tall. He was wearing a derby hat and a walking suit. I says to myself, Archie, you're in the wrong line of work if the bleeding coppers—no disrespect intended, Inspector—make the coin to dress like that on the job."

"And his shoes?"

"Didn't see much of them, I'm afraid. He was wearing spats."

Holmes and I shared a glance, and the look in his eye told me to say no more. We continued down the hallway as Lestrade berated Hennessey and warned him that if he ever let another person gander at a body under investigation without his say so, he'd lock him in a cell with a few of his customers and forget where he left the key.

"Damned newsmen." Lestrade continued his tirade. "Worse yet, the bounder might have been an artist here to sketch the mayhem. And forged credentials to boot! Bloody hell! I'll watch the papers this week, and if I see a picture of Porter in one I'll hang the sketcher by his thumbs."

"Here we are, gentlemen." Archie pushed open a wide door and stepped aside for us to enter. I've been in emergency surgeries and triage hospitals with all of their hectic bustle and urgency, but neither awes me so much as an operating theatre where Death in every form is displayed in all its crimson and ebon glory and contemplated in quiet repose.

Because Saint Mark's is a teaching hospital, the floor of their theatre housed ten or more cadavers at the time, all reclining on steel drain tables and covered with white canvas sheets, specimens for students to dissect.

My gaze swept the ranks of empty seats in the shadowed gallery and I recalled the many times I had sat in seats just like them while the mysteries of human anatomy were laid on a table like so many vegetables at a market, weighed and jugged and labeled or put back again. "Here's our boy over here." Archie gestured to a gurney against the wall away from the door. He took a corner of the sheet between his thumb and forefinger and playing to an empty house with a flourish worthy of Robert-Houdin at the Saint James Theatre, whisked it away.

"I'd venture to say, sirs that our friend Porter here is such damaged goods that even old Burke and Hare couldn't sell him."

Hennessey's jest was no exaggeration. The rats had been sufficiently numerous and had enough time to gnaw away the greater part of Porter's face, hands, and throat, those parts of him that were openly exposed. Some of the more enterprising beggars had burrowed under his shirt and feasted on the soft tissues of his entrails.

"Do you have gloves, Hennessey?" With my

hands safely covered, I took his left foot by the ankle and raised the leg. His calf was shy a large chunk of its muscle. "Bleeders went right up his trouser leg, they did," Archie cackled.

Before I could strip off the gloves, Holmes called to me. "Here, Watson. Have a look at this." Holmes pointed to the torn flesh of the throat. I pulled away the tattered skin and examined the larynx. It had been crushed, and taking into account the thickness of Porter's neck, I could see that it was a powerful hand that did the job.

"So, Holmes," said Lestrade. "It was murder, after all."

Hennessey's eyebrows raised. "Holmes? Sherlock Holmes? In my theatre? Ha!" Hennessey practically danced with glee. "Wait'll I tell my mates at the pub."

Lestrade clamped his hand roughly on Hennessey's chin. And turned his bulging eyes to look straight into Lestrade's glare. "You'll tell no one any such thing. You'll keep your flap shut, or I'll have you up on charges for interfering with an investigation. Do we understand?" Hennessey's head bobbed in agreement. "Good man. Now take our friend Mr. Porter somewhere away from prying eyes, won't you?" Hennessey nodded again, and Lestrade shoved him away. "See that he does, Sergeant. Holmes, Watson, it's time you go home."

We were back in our lodgings before I broached the subject. "I noticed something significant about Porter's calf."

Holmes had lit a match. He held it over the bowl of his pipe and smiled. "I wondered whether you saw the same thing I did."

"Some of the tooth marks looked to be made with chisels rather than with awls, and too large for rats. I served in Afghanistan, Holmes. I know the work of a cannibal when I see it."

***

I slept poorly that night. Holmes was still sitting in his chair when I went to bed after three and there still, with a heap of books and papers at either hand when I wakened at nine. "I had Mrs. Hudson delay breakfast until you were up and about," he said. "Did you sleep well?"

"You're joking," I said, "what with the thought of a cannibal running lose in the city."

"We've had them before. Remember that Jack the Ripper claimed he fried and ate a victim's kidney."

"How could I forget? Especially anticipating breakfast."

At this moment Mrs. Hudson entered with the breakfast tray.

"You know, Watson, there are three fundamental reasons for cannibalism: famine, intimidation, and sympathetic magic."

Mrs. Hudson went wide-eyed at this point and stared at nothing in particular as she set the dishes out as quickly as possible. She exited in quite a hurry.

"Magic?" I said, sawing at a link of sausage with my table knife.

"Yes, Watson. Many primitive tribes believe

that eating the flesh of an individual imparts his or her characteristics to the eater. In the same way many native tribes in America believe that eating the heart of a deer, say, imbues the person with great speed. There are tribes that eat the hearts of those they have killed in battle to absorb their strengths or skills. Some extend the practice to eating their captives for the same reason. Intimidation comes into play when conquerors extend the practice to a conquered tribe to frighten them into submission while reducing their numbers to prevent resistance."

"And our phantom in the tunnels?"

"Most likely hunger drove him to kill Porter because his food supply was curtailed."

"The rats."

"Yes, the rats," Holmes said, his enthusiasm rising. "Porter complained that someone was opening the traps and freeing his catches. Perhaps the killer was robbing the traps instead."

"And Porter caught him at it; a fight ensued, and bereft of his rats the killer made do with the rat catcher."

Holmes dug into his black pudding with great gusto. I left mine untouched, favouring the eggs. "There is perhaps one further reason for cannibalism, Holmes," I said, "long standing custom."

Holmes looked up from his plate. "Watson, that is an excellent observation, someone from a place where cannibalism is a standard practice transplanted here and forced to revert. An immigrant, perhaps or someone visiting and forced into dire circumstances."

"You then dismiss the possibility that the killer may be other than human?"

"The shape of the footprints we saw preclude Dupin's orangutan, if that's what you are thinking. The toes were not prehensile. So combining factors we must seek a person small in stature but possessing great strength and agility whose origin is a culture in which cannibalism is common. Perhaps a circus performer, an acrobat or high wire artist."

"Or a sideshow dwarf?"

"Possibly, since dwarves are usually proportional to common people, simply smaller in scale, but such a person would have to be extraordinarily strong to have killed Porter bare handed."

Mrs. Hudson knocked on the door. "A message for you, Mr. Holmes, from Inspector Lestrade; a carriage is waiting downstairs." She handed Holmes the paper and he read it silently. "Dress quickly, Watson. Our presence is required at the Yard."

I hesitated. "So tell me, Holmes, when do we share our thoughts with the Inspector?"

"As soon as we are sure that we don't send him climbing the wrong rope."

As I dressed, I couldn't help but feel that Holmes's reticence to tell Lestrade of our theories was influenced by the puzzle of our anonymous correspondent. I have always trusted Holmes implicitly, but on this occasion, I felt that he was more interested in solving the riddle of the letter in Chapman's *Homer* than he was in catching Porter's killer.

***

Early that morning Lestrade and his men had gone into the Underground to round up as many of the tunnel dwellers, the desperate homeless souls who squatted in the nooks and crannies of the tubes, as they could find. When we arrived at Scotland Yard, we found a good score of them waiting in a room off the lobby.

They were a scrofulous lot, unwashed and clad in multiple layers of ragged clothing against the winter chill. At a quick glance I saw signs among them of rickets, scurvy, scabies and general malnutrition. I would guess that all of their teeth put together wouldn't have made a full set.

"I say, Holmes, there doesn't seem to be any among the lost strong enough to kill a fly let alone a man Porter's size."

"We won't find our killer among these poor folk, but one of them may contribute to our understanding. Even the poor and ignorant have their story to tell."

A bobby, his crisp uniform and shiny brass buttons a sharp contrast to the ragged mob, appeared at a doorway and summoned us inside. Lestrade and Shepperton sat at a table with a chair before it and two chairs flanking theirs on the other side.

"Quite a convention you have outside, Inspector," Holmes said.

"I had to take what I could find. Work has stopped on the tunnel while we comb that bloody labyrinth looking for the killer. I've never seen such a hodgepodge of cuts and clefts and passages going every which way.

"The railway bigwigs are leaning on the Commissioner for us to let the workers back in, and the Commissioner's leaning on me to solve the case. My men and I grabbed up this lot in the wee hours and brought them here for questioning although Heaven knows what I'll do with them when we're done."

Holmes asked, "Will Webb be joining us?"

Lestrade scowled. "That man is an infernal nuisance. He demands we let him run his own show, and it's all we can do to keep him and his pack of head breakers out of the place."

I half expected Holmes to somehow inveigle Lestrade into changing his attitude, but instead he said simply, "How may we help you in this effort, Inspector?"

"You've seen all that I have in this business," he began.

But you haven't seen all that we have, Lestrade, I thought.

He continued. "I'm under pressure to solve this case and quickly. I'm hoping you may catch something in what these blighters have to say that will speed that end." He turned to a bobby standing by the door. "Perkins, bring in the first of the lot."

The first three of the vagrants were typical of the human detritus that made a life in London's nether regions. Addled by cheap gin, their testimony verged on incoherence, and I was starting to think that we were wasting our time until the fourth tunnel dweller, a scrawny fellow named Wiggins, said something the others did not.

Wiggins wore a threadbare greatcoat over what looked like three shirts nesting one inside the next. His dun cloth cap lay in his lap and he persisted in running his hand over his baldpate as if it still had hair.

"Begging your pardon, Inspector," he said, tugging nervously at his long, drooping moustache, "but you've got your head in the wrong rain barrel, so to speak of. Weren't none of us poor folk what killed old Porter. We all knowed him, and we got along. Live and let live, I say. It's the ghost what done it."

Lestrade heaved an exasperated sigh. "Ghosts. Balderdash."

"No, sir," said Wiggins indignantly. "Not at all. I seen him with these two eyes." He pointed to them with his forked fingers.

"Perkins, get this fool out of here."

Holmes had been silent to this point. He leaned forward and held up his hand. "Wait." He turned to Lestrade. "Let us hear him out." Lestrade opened his mouth to protest but Holmes cut him off. "Mr. Wiggins, where did you see this ghost?"

"In one of the cross tunnels away from the one they're digging right now. It was a few days ago, three, maybe four, and I was slipping in from a day's scavenging behind the pubs. Got to watch out for the railroad police, you do. They act as they're paid for, I suppose; it's them grand nabobs what runs the City and South who got no sympathy for a poor old veteran of the Fifth Northumberland

Fusiliers where I served the Empire and the Queen, God bless her."

"For pity's sake, man, get to the point," Lestrade growled.

"Please, Inspector, let him tell his story," said Holmes.

"Thank you kindly, sir," said Wiggins. "I can tell you're quality. You respects a man's dignity even when he's fallen on bad times. As I was saying, I had to duck and slink to get past the rail coppers and on to my barrow, and near where they're digging now I heard two of them coming and I ducked into that little side passage I mentioned. It was there I seen him. The ghost."

"Please describe the ghost for us, Mr. Wiggins," Holmes said.

"I thought at first he was far away because of his eyes. Glowed in the dark they did like that bobby's buttons over there. Then my own lamps adjusted for a better look and I seen the dim shape of him and understood that his eyes wasn't far away but close to the ground. A man he looked like, short but thick, squat if you will. Then the eyes winked out, and I turned and ran, afraid he'd show up on the other side of me and trap me in that tunnel."

"Have you seen him since?" I interjected.

"No, sir, I ain't and grateful for it."

Holmes put a sovereign on the table between them and pushed it toward Wiggins. "I want you to do something for me, Mr. Wiggins." Holmes kept his finger on the coin.

"Name it, sir," Wiggins said, eyeing the money.

"No man who has served as you have deserves

such a lot as yours. I want you to take this coin, and use it to get yourself a bath and a shave, some clean clothes and a good meal, but mind you, no liquor." Holmes laid his card on the table beside the sovereign. "You are to report to this address no later than six tomorrow evening that I may see that you have followed my instructions. I have a job for you." Holmes's voice became stern. "Give me your word."

Wiggins nodded and held up his right hand. "My word, sir, you have it." My instincts told me that not only was Wiggins sincere in his promise but that he would keep it.

"Good man. Inspector, do you have further questions?"

"No." Lestrade's voice betrayed his irritation with both Wiggins and Holmes.

Holmes took his finger from the coin. Wiggins stood and picked it up. He stared at it as if he were afraid it would vanish from his fingers. He turned to leave and Holmes said, "One more thing, Mr. Wiggins." The fellow turned back to face us. "Yes, sir?"

"As you value your life, stay out of the tunnels." Holmes's change of tone gave me a chill as I am certain it did Wiggins. He nodded somberly. "Yes, sir, I shall."

The remaining tunnel people offered nothing useful or remarkable. Lestrade released them with a stern warning to stay out of the Underground on penalty of arrest. On the carriage ride back to Baker Street I asked Holmes, "What was that business with Wiggins all about?"

THE AFFAIR OF THE CHRONIC ARGONAUT

"I wished to ensure that the man did not return to the tunnels, Watson. If he does, we might not find him again. He is the only person thus far who may have seen our killer, and that makes the Underground doubly dangerous for him."

"Then why not have Lestrade lock him up, put him in protective custody?"

"If he were locked in the Old Bailey we would have to do hand springs and cartwheels to speak with him again. Further, I believe we will have to go into those tunnels once more before this affair is over, and I also believe our Mr. Wiggins knows them well, perhaps even better than Superintendent Webb."

"So you give his tale credence, a ghost with glowing eyes? Really, Holmes. Human eyes don't shine in the dark."

"Ordinary humans, Watson, lack the *tapetum lucidum*, the layer of tissue in the eye found in many vertebrates that allows what we call 'eyeshine.' Yet I am sure you will agree that our killer is anything but ordinary."

The weak sun that shone through a grey curtain of cloud did little to mitigate the bitter cold, and I was glad to return to the fire in our sitting room. Put in the mood by Wiggins's tale, I was reading a ghost story by one E.H. Begbie in the December edition of Pall Mall magazine, and Holmes was seated in his customary chair with a book on his lap.

"What's that you're reading, Holmes?"

"Re-reading, Watson; *On the Origin of Species*."

"Darwin? Indeed. I thought that controversy had

faded away long since."

"It has faded, Watson, yet I believe it will rise again. There will be dissension and dispute so long as two humans exist to have private opinions."

"Creation versus evolution," I said. "An irreconcilable issue."

"My interest in Darwin's theories lies less in the theological realm than it does in the practical."

"In what way?" Before Holmes could answer, Mrs. Hudson knocked at the door. "A message for you, Mr. Holmes."

"Who delivered it, Mrs. Hudson?"

"A rag-tag little fellow, couldn't have been a day older than ten years." Holmes rushed to the window, threw open the sash and put his head out to scan the street one way then the other. "Blast," said Holmes. "No sight of him."

"Shall we go out and look for the boy?" I suggested.

Holmes shook his head. "No, Watson, I fear the City has swallowed him." He turned to Mrs. Hudson. "Thank you. If any messenger brings something for me over the next few days, please ask him to wait; tell him there's a bob in it for him if he does."

"Yes, sir, I'll do that." She left and Holmes held up the envelope, an envelope with his name written in the same precise lettering as the last.

"Watson, please close the window."

***

Holmes studied the envelope for a good five

minutes before he opened it. I was ready to snatch it from his hands and open it myself, my curiosity burned so. He read the note inside and laid it on the table. As he crossed to the bookshelves, I read: The consulting detective might deign to consult *Hamlet* I: v., 188-9.

Holmes drew a volume from its shelf and spread it open on the table. He thumbed through the book until he found the second envelope tucked between the pages. Holmes didn't hesitate but slit the envelope straight away. There was neither stamp nor address on it. He unfolded the sheet inside and flattened it on the table beside its companion.

"What time is it, Watson?"

"Half past five."

"We have less than five hours to save a life."

I stared at the message. It read: Chauncey Courtland will be murdered on the evening of the 15th November, 1899 at ten o'clock.

Holmes carefully folded the letter and slipped it back into the envelope.

"Holmes, it's time we took this to Scotland Yard."

His brow folded into lines of thought. "Yes, Watson, time indeed." His finger fell on the passage from Shakespeare and he read aloud, " 'The time is out of joint—O cursed spite, that ever I was born to set it right.' Do you recognise the passage, Watson?"

"It's Hamlet speaking, is it not?"

"Yes, on the heels of meeting his father's ghost. Our dilemma is clear, Watson. If we present this letter to Scotland Yard, we shall have to explain its significance in the light of its predecessor and be charged with interference in a murder investigation. Lestrade would likely have us incarcerated and prevent us from investigating the case further. If we do not present the letter, we run the risk of allowing another murder. Since the previous prediction proved accurate, that is a substantial risk."

"You know what I think already, Holmes. Take the letter to Lestrade."

"Let us be logical, Watson. If we do so, what will Lestrade do that we cannot?"

"He can bring the entire force of Scotland Yard to bear on the problem."

"But can he, Watson? Could he pull every constable from his regular beat to search all of London, seine six and a half million people, for one man? And even if he did, to coordinate the search and instruct them would take until midnight by itself and if our unknown correspondent is correct, Chauncey Courtland will already be dead. You and I could conduct a focused search with far more likelihood of success—quality versus quantity."

"But Holmes, where would we begin?"

"We begin by coordinating what we know." Holmes began filling his pipe. "Our mysterious correspondent is becoming increasingly confident. He began by mailing a message to himself under a pseudonym then concealing it here, apparently with some modicum of leisure, since he knew that I had a specific volume in my library. That missive foretold Porter's murder but would not be found until after the fact. The intent, I believe, was to establish his credibility.

THE AFFAIR OF THE CHRONIC ARGONAUT

"This time he has dispensed with the mailing of the message and has directly planted it in another book. And this time, he has foretold a murder before it will occur, knowing that now we will take his forecast seriously. He has presented us with a challenge, Watson, and if we are to save a life, we are bound to meet it."

"And how do you propose that we do so?"

"It seems to me that our correspondent either has chosen Chauncey Courtland as his victim or that he is privy to some plot on his life. If I understand his nature correctly, he would not give us a puzzle we could not solve. I suggest that we get to work post-haste on its solution. Bring your revolver, Watson. There is no telling how this evening may end."

In moments we were on the street hailing a cab. As we climbed in, Holmes told the driver, "The British Museum, as quickly as possible."

In the cab to Bloomsbury, Holmes sat silent. I interrupted his thoughts by saying, "Is it of no concern to you, Holmes, that our quarters have been entered, twice now, and we have no idea how that was done?"

"It is very much a concern to me, Watson, and I realise it is an integral part of this whole affair, but at the moment it is secondary to the saving of Chauncey Courtland's life."

"It all seems like an elaborate parlour trick to me," I grumbled.

Holmes turned to me and fixed me with a stare. "That is an interesting observation, Watson, and it may open an entire new line of investigation once we've gotten past the matter at hand. But first, Chauncey Courtland."

***

The great Round Reading room of the British Museum was as still as a tomb, save for an occasional shuffling of papers or muted cough. Holmes had procured reader's tickets for us both long before, as his investigations and curious pursuits led him again and again to the greatest font of information since the Library of Alexandria. This time, however, the search was for the most mundane of subjects.

I'm not certain what persuasion Holmes may have used, but I suspect that his reputation was instrumental in procuring our permission to browse the stacks instead of the customary filling out of a request ticket for each volume, and we soon found ourselves in the labyrinthine shelving of hundreds of thousands of books. The stacks stood three floors high with catwalks and railings, surprisingly well lit. A hawk-faced reference librarian who wore pince-nez spectacles on his blade of a nose guided us to the section that contained the business and professional directories and stood watch the entire time we were there as if we would steal something or tear a page from one of the volumes to light a cigar.

I found the first Chauncey Courtland, a barrister with an office and a separate residential address in Knightsbridge. Holmes found a second, an importer operating from the docks whose home was in

THE AFFAIR OF THE CHRONIC ARGONAUT

King's Cross. He also found the third, a butcher with a shop in Clapham.

Holmes knelt and spread a sheet of paper on the floor. Peering over his shoulder, I saw a map of the existing Underground with the plan of the current excavation pencilled in. As I watched, he marked Xs on the map.

Time intruded. The closing hour approached and we were harrumphed from the stacks by our proctor and all but marched out the door. Our cab was waiting, for Holmes had given the driver a five-pound note to engage him for the evening. "Clapham," he told the driver, "and hurry."

"Why Clapham, Holmes?"

"Think, Watson. The tunnel excavations are near Clapham, and the lines have a large junction and station there. Further, we've established hunger as a likely motive for our carnivorous killer. Where better to seek him out than a shambles?"

It would have been a close race to arrive at Clapham before ten o'clock under ordinary circumstances, but a fire near Spitalfields Market forced our driver to circumnavigate half of London, it seemed, before we were back on track again. We arrived at the Kent Street address of Courtland Meats at seven minutes after ten.

The shop was dark, as was the residence overhead. Holmes and I pressed our faces to the glass of the pavement window. Inside, a shadowy figure was moving behind the counter. It turned, and I almost cried out at the sight of a pair of glowing eyes. Holmes put his shoulder to the door and after three tries it flew open, crashing into the wall behind it. The intruder was gone but Chauncey Courtland was not.

The butcher lay dead on his back behind the counter. He was wearing a sleeping shirt that was pulled up nearly to his hip where his left leg had been crudely hacked off. A bloody cleaver lay on the floor beside him. I knelt and felt vainly at his throat for a pulse. "He's still warm." Holmes ran to the back of the shop but soon returned. "A window to the alley is broken. Our killer is gone."

A light shone through the door. A bobby on rounds noticed the open door and had come to investigate. "Here now, what's all this?" He came round the counter and when he shone his lantern on Courtland's bloody corpse immediately blew his whistle.

***

Biggs, the officer who had come into the shop, went from trepidation at confronting two possible murderers to relief when Holmes and I identified ourselves. With the shop lit, I could see at once that Courtland was dead before his limb was severed. The blood pooled below his hip would have pumped out faster and farther had he still been alive. Like Porter, his throat was crushed, the strangler's marks in his flesh.

"It's definitely our killer, Watson." Holmes pointed to a bloody bare footprint on the floor. "The glass from the broken window is on the floor inside, so it was broken from the alley and the window then used as an entry. Apparently the noise roused

Courtland from his slumber and he came downstairs to investigate, perhaps with that cleaver in his hand. He was overpowered and strangled then the killer hacked off the leg. Apparently he took it with him."

"But why cut off the butcher's leg in the middle of a shop full of meat?"

"I have come to think, Watson, that it is a preference."

***

Within an hour, Lestrade and a coterie of officers arrived on the scene. He and Sergeant Shepperton pushed their way through the crowd that had gathered outside, stretching their necks for a look through Courtland's shop window. He conferred with Biggs, periodically glaring at us over the constable's shoulder. By the time he spoke to us, his face was flushed with anger.

"All right, Holmes. Biggs tells me that you were here while the body was still warm. What prevents me from having you cuffed right now?" We were fortunate that Holmes had engaged the cabbie for the evening, as he was able to corroborate the time when we arrived.

"Some explanation is in order, Inspector. Watson and I received an anonymous communication threatening Mr. Courtland's life, and we hurried here with all dispatch."

"And you didn't think to alert the Yard?"

"We are talking life and death. We had to locate this place and get here as quickly as possible. I only regret that we were too late to save Courtland.

However, we did get a look at the killer, albeit a poor one."

Holmes recounted seeing the shadowy figure behind the counter and his flight as we broke in the door, leaving out the detail of his shining eyes. "So," said Lestrade, "You found the murderer in the act, did you?"

"Yes, Inspector, and to my regret, we arrived too late to apprehend him."

"Inspector," Shepperton called from the doorway. "We found the leg."

Lestrade said, "Don't you dare leave here, Holmes. I'm far from through with you yet."

"I wouldn't dream of leaving, Inspector. In fact I'm going to stay right beside you. Let us go see what your man has found. Come along, Watson."

Lestrade opened his mouth to protest then abandoned the idea. Two blocks over in a dark alley, Courtland's leg lay on the cobblestones to one side behind a dustbin. "I wouldn't have noticed it, sir," the bobby, a short fellow named Shanks, told Lestrade, "but for the dogs worrying at it. A pack of mongrels of every sort."

"How many dogs, constable?" said Holmes.

"I don't see what this has to do with—" Lestrade began.

"It was hard to tell in all the confusion, Mr. Holmes," said Shanks, ignoring Lestrade. "Six, maybe eight. I had to use my billy to break them up. A tenacious lot they was."

"And did you kill that one?" Holmes pointed to a black and white furred heap on the other side of the alley.

The bobby peered into the shadows. "No, sir. I just knocked them a bit and set them running."

"That'll be all, Shanks," said Lestrade dismissively. I knelt beside the leg and trained my lamp on it. "Holmes, give me your glass." I studied the flesh as carefully as I could but found only the marks of canine teeth. "Only dogs, Holmes."

"Well what did you think you might find?" huffed Lestrade.

Holmes eyed him coldly. "Inspector, have you stopped to ponder why Courtland's leg was lopped off and carried away?"

Lestrade offered no response, so Holmes continued. "Our killer appears to be a cannibal."

Lestrade's eyes blazed. "You'll stop that talk right now, Holmes, or I'll put you in a cell. I'll not have you inciting panic."

Holmes smiled grimly. "Count your lucky stars, Lestrade, that this did not occur in Whitechapel."

Lestrade turned to his men. "Wrap that damned thing," he said pointing at Courtland's leg, "and bring it along. Don't let that rabble out front see it." He stormed off with his retinue in tow, leaving us alone in the alley.

"None so blind, Watson," said Holmes. "A pack of feral dogs on the scent of blood can be as savage as wolves. Though he killed one dog, there apparently were too many of them for our murderer to defend his prize and escape at the same time. Why a leg and not an arm? He is laying in provisions. I have no doubt that our man will kill again and soon."

***

I am not certain whether the scratchy moan of Holmes's violin woke me or it was simply the first thing I heard. I found him sawing away at it by the window. The weather had broken overnight and for the first day in a week, morning sun shone through the glass.

"Watson," he called over the droning notes, "good that you're about. Please ring Mrs. Hudson to bring up the breakfast. We have things to discuss."

Holmes was worrying at a slice of ham with his knife when he said something I am unaccustomed to hearing: "I've been foolish, Watson. I've allowed a prejudice to interfere with my thinking."

"What prejudice might that be, Holmes?"

He held up his hand pointing the fork with the bite of ham on it for emphasis. "What I believed to be impossible. I am afraid I must revise my catalogue." He spoke around his bite of ham. "You saying last night that the whole business seemed like some parlour trick jogged my memory. Some time ago, Watson, you told me a story. That friend of yours who writes the fantastic novels, Wells, took you to with him to dinner at the home of a friend of his, an inventor, I believe."

"You mean Willoughby? That humbug. Hard to take the man seriously; he was always playing some elaborate prank or another. How was it that Wells described the fellow? Hard to see all around the man. Should have been a stage magician, that one; too clever to be believed on his face."

"You told me that Willoughby demonstrated a

THE AFFAIR OF THE CHRONIC ARGONAUT

device that evening."

"A 'time machine' he called it. A pretty little gadget, all brass and copper and clockwork with a few gemstones and bits of ivory here and there. He set it on the table, said some claptrap about moving through time as a fourth dimension. A lever on the machine was pressed and it simply vanished in a puff of air. Even blew out a nearby candle; magicians use things like that for distraction."

"Yes, Watson, misdirection they call it."

"Quite. Well, you know how fond I am of stage magicians, Holmes. I've seen the best of the lot, but this was as good a trick as ever I've seen. I'll be blasted if I could see how he did it. Willoughby staunchly denied it was trick; then he took us to his workshop and showed us a larger unfinished model of the same machine. I thought he was perhaps building the larger one to sell. I'd wager Bailey and Tripp would pay a pretty penny for the plans. Willoughby said that he intended to use the device to travel through time.

"To perpetuate the hoax, he invited us to dinner again the following week and showed up all dishevelled with some incredible fable of going into the future in the machine and returning, just in time for dinner. Wells wrote his first novel about it."

"And Willoughby?"

"That's the strange item, Holmes; soon after that evening, he dropped out of sight and hasn't been around in quite some time. Blank the editor said he thought he saw him crossing Grosvenor Square a few months ago and called to him, but the fellow moved on. Knowing Willoughby's prankish nature,

I half expect him to appear at dinner some evening as if he'd just stepped out for some cigars. Just another of his tricks."

Holmes was silent for a moment then shook his table knife at me. "But, Watson, what if it were not a trick? What if his machine were real?"

My fork stopped halfway to my mouth. "Surely, Holmes, you can't believe—"

"How many times I have said, Watson, when you eliminate the impossible…"

"Whatever remains must be the truth. Yes, yes, Holmes."

"I believe that what we have thought to be impossible may have been demonstrated otherwise." Holmes took his pipe to his favourite chair. "You have a copy of Wells's novel, do you not?" I crossed to the bookshelves and after some searching found the slim volume. I opened the cover and read the inscription on the flyleaf: to my good friend John Watson, H. G. Wells., signed with that flamboyant penmanship and built in colophon he affected since fame had betaken him. I handed Holmes *The Time Machine*, and he was silent for the rest of the morning.

Just before lunch, Holmes closed the book. "Watson, you have read this, have you not?"

"Well yes, when it was first published."

"Do you remember its details?"

"Enough of it, I suppose."

"How accurately does it depict the attitudes of the Time Traveller's guests at the telling of his tale?"

"The scepticism? Absolutely so. We all believed

it to be a marvellous bit of play-acting on Willoughby's part, quite creative. I dare say none of us believed a word, for as I told you, the man was notorious for playing jokes."

"I too am sceptical. I prefer to deal in fact, but let us be speculative for a moment. In the novel, the Time Traveller, Willoughby if you will, goes into the future and returns to the present. He arrives a week after the time of his departure. What if he had arrived instead a week before?

"Based on what we have before us I am beginning to believe that not only was Willoughby successful, but that he has continued his experiments. Let us consider the unalterable nature of causality, the foundation of the scientific method. Once a thing is done, it cannot be undone. What if that were no longer true?"

"No longer true? How can that be, Holmes?"

"You would agree, would you not, Watson, that Time may be defined as follows: an agreed standard of measurement predicated on human perception of celestial movement and biochemical reactivity?"

"Well, yes, in a manner of speaking," I said. "But it seems too simple to define it in that fashion."

"I admit the definition is reductive, but for the purpose of discussion, it should be adequate. You acknowledge that all objects in the Universe exist in three dimensions, do you not?"

"Of course; height, width and depth."

"If you think of Time as a fourth dimension, an occupational one, it all makes sense; not only where an object exists, but when." Holmes set his pipe on the table. "My pipe exists in this place at this time. Agreed?"

"Yes, but—"

"And if I move it through one of the three dimensions," he raised it from the table, "it no longer exists in that specific space although it still exists at this time."

"Of course it does, Holmes. What's the point?"

"The point, my dear fellow, is that while I am moving it through the three spatial dimensions, the pipe is moving forward through the fourth as well. We don't notice it because we too are moving in the same temporal direction at precisely the same speed. Like my pipe, you and I exist in the present, and the present is now. And now." He paused for a moment. "And now."

He leaned forward and cocked his head. "But what if I were able to push my pipe some distance forward in time faster than the ordinary flow?" I didn't answer because I confess that at this point, I was absolutely perplexed. "Watson, it would not exist in the present with us, until time moved us forward and we caught up with it."

"Caught up with it? I don't follow you."

"I shall use another analogy. Let us say you and I are floating down a river on a raft. I dive off the raft and swim to shore then run ahead faster than the river's speed. A mile downriver, I stop and wait. Shortly, the river will bring the raft to my location and I can rejoin you."

"Well, yes, Holmes, that is obvious."

"If then time like that river flows in one direction at a fixed rate, Watson, what if I had a conveyance that would allow me to leave the stream and run at a higher speed along the bank? I could arrive in the future ahead of you."

"Holmes, this is giving me a blasted headache."

He ignored me and went on, caught up in uncharacteristic enthusiasm. "And what if that conveyance could take me backward against the natural flow? Could I go back into the past and sink the raft before we ever departed? Or substitute a canoe or a rowboat? In other words, could I change what has already happened?"

"Holmes, this is sheer poppycock. The past is the past and cannot be changed. What's done is done."

"We would like to think so, but what we have experienced has to have been accomplished either by sorcery or by some heretofore unsuspected scientific machination. I am inclined to choose the latter. Up to now, we have operated on the premise that our correspondent is either the murderer or the murderer's accomplice because he knows the identity of the victim and even the time of the event in advance. Thus he can leave us his communiqués to set us in motion."

"But how?"

"Given the opportunity, he can find the means. And if he fails on one occasion, he may use his conveyance to return and try again."

"Surely you don't plan to broach this notion with Lestrade."

Holmes snorted. "If your intellect struggles with the concept, how do you suppose Lestrade would manage it?"

I put my fingers to my aching temples. "Then you think Willoughby is the murderer, playing some game of fox-and-geese with us?"

"No, Watson, but I do believe that Willoughby, our correspondent, and the bearded man in the spats are one and the same. It is time we went to Richmond."

***

We arrived just after noon at Willoughby's address to find his grand old house boarded up and falling into disrepair. The untended gardens were a riot of rose bushes and thistles competing for dominance. A limb had fallen from one of the elms and lay across the walk to the front door.

"Apparently Willoughby has not returned," I said.

Holmes stood silent studying the scene then said. "That may be so, or it may not." Holmes called to a pair of boys up the block scooping up what snow they could find to build a puny snowman. They crossed the street looking more warily at the house than at us. "Hello, lads," Holmes said. "Can you tell me who lives in this house?"

"No one lives there, sir, said the taller one, a dark eyed boy in a short leather jacket and knit cap. Stood empty a few years, it has."

"A fine house like that? I should think someone would move into it in no time."

The other boy spoke up. He was a tow-headed youngster missing both his front teeth. That gave him a prominent lisp that made his sentence almost unintelligible. "That's because it's haunted, sir."

"Haunted? Indeed."

Both boys nodded with wide-eyed alacrity. "Sometimes at night there's noises and strange lights inside," said the dark-haired boy.

"Does this happen every night?"

"No, sir," said the tow-head, "only once or twice that I heard of, and I never saw it myself."

"And you have never set foot in the place?"

"Oh, no, sir. I'm too scared."

"Tell them about Robert and Tommy," said his companion.

"One night this summer," the tow head said, "two of the neighbour boys Robert Caruthers and Tommy Morgan went inside—on a dare, you know? They found a loose board around back and climbed through a window. They weren't in the house five minutes when the ghost tells them, 'Get out. Get out or die.' They said his voice come from every room at once. They scarpered out of there, and nobody's gone in since."

"Quite a story." Holmes pulled two shillings from his pocket and gave one to each of the boys. "Good lads. Run along now."

When the boys were out of earshot, Holmes said. "You said Willoughby was fond of pranks. Was he also fond of ghosts?"

"Now that you say it, Holmes, I recall one occasion when one appeared in the middle of Christmas dinner and startled us all. I'm sure it was a contrivance Willoughby rigged up, another of his stunts but he neither explained nor admitted it. What are you getting at?"

"Ghosts, Watson. Ghosts in the underground; ghosts in the abandoned mansion. What better way to frighten off the unduly curious?"

We wrestled the rusted gate open and picked our way through a tangle of weeds to the rear of the house. The porch off the kitchen was shielded by a wall to one side and a trellis of roses to the other. The windows were soundly boarded over. If there were a loose board before, it had been since repaired. Holmes opened his pocketknife and began digging at a good-sized knot in the pine planking. The plug removed, he put an eye to the peephole.

"Have a look, Watson."

Little light filtered through gaps in the boards, but I was able to see the kitchen table and on it a plate, a mug and a candlestick with a burned down candle. Then something dark moved quickly over the table and down to the floor. It was a mouse.

"Food on the table recent enough to still be feeding a rodent, Watson." We found a cellar door that wasn't boarded over under storm shutters and after a few minutes of worrying at the lock, Holmes had it open. The cellar was lightless save for what came through the doorway. Holmes struck a match and cast about until he found a candle. By its flickering glow we found our way through the maze of cellar rooms.

Most of them were filled with clutter, some of the type one might find in any old house; broken furniture, old trunks and such. Other items were more interesting. We saw pieces of mechanism, gears and springs, and electrical and chemical apparatus among other trappings of the inventor's trade. In some rooms we found devices at whose purpose we could only guess; unfulfilled dreams of Willoughby's creative genius.

Then we found the cage.

It was a stout contrivance made of half inch steel bars and stood six feet high by eight by eight. Its door was ajar, an open padlock lying on the floor beside it. Inside were a pallet, an open keg of water and a tin plate with a spoiled leg of lamb on it. Flies buzzed around the plate like bees at a honeycomb.

"Watson, are you armed?"

I patted the pocket of my greatcoat. My old service-revolver was still there from the previous evening. "Yes."

"Then let us go upstairs and see what more we may find."

The house was still, so much so that I started at any creak or pop in its old boards. The boarded windows let in little more than twilight despite the bright sun outdoors. The plate on the kitchen table had only a crust of bread and a handful of boiled beans on it, and the mug held the sticky residue of wine.

"See what you can find down here, Watson. I will look in the upper floors."

The parlour and dining room, which were familiar to me from previous visits, now looked foreboding with their shrouded furniture and film of dust on every surface. I caught my eye twitching as if to catch one of the shrouds rising like some spectre in a Mrs. Gaskell story, but nothing stirred. I was about to move down the hallway to the annex where Willoughby had his workshop when I heard a deep sepulchral voice say, "Get out. Get out or die."

I pulled my pistol from my pocket and whirled one way and another looking for the source of the voice but saw no one. "Get out," it echoed, seeming to come from every room in the house. Then I heard Holmes's voice with the same reverberation say, "Watson, come upstairs and see what I've found."

Holmes stood at the foot of a great canopied bed in what must have been the master bedroom. The first thing I noticed was that the dust cover was pulled back and the bedclothes turned down at an angle on one side only.

The wardrobe stood open and in it I saw a rank of suits, shirts and jackets, Willoughby's clothing. "Wherever our friend has gone, Watson, he seems to have packed little in his trunk." Holmes crossed to a chiffonier in a far corner. "Look closely, Watson. It is ingenious. See where the mirror frame attaches to the chest? Concealed hinges."

Holmes pulled the mirror frame forward revealing a brass funnel set flat into the wall. He leaned into it and said, "Get out. Get out or die." The words rang all over the house. "A speaking tube, Watson, linked to every room and so extensive that it echoes like a mine shaft. There's your ghost. Our friend Willoughby is a very clever fellow. Let us see what else he has contrived."

The workshop off the first floor of Willoughby's house was a large single room with a tall ceiling inset with skylights that made it very bright in comparison to the rest of the house. Its end opened into the garden that occupied the north side of the property. Workbenches lined both walls and an array of tools hung on hooks. The centre of the room was empty.

"This is where Willoughby showed you the large machine?"

"Yes. This is his workshop. The machine sat right there."

Holmes browsed the workbenches and picked up a pair of leather bound journals he found lying on one. He pulled a chair to one side of the room. He sat and began thumbing through one of the volumes.

"Holmes," I said, "what are you doing?"

"Waiting," he said.

"Waiting for what?"

"If I am correct, something extraordinary. I suggest you find a chair, Watson, we may be here for a while."

The afternoon sun passed overhead and it was nearly four o'clock when I became aware of an odd humming. The very air in the workshop seemed to vibrate.

I watched amazed as a form came into view, insubstantial at first, shimmering like a reflection on a rippling pond. The image came into focus and I recognised Willoughby's machine. Seated in its saddle with his hands on the controls was our bearded friend in the derby.

He looked at us and seemed as startled as we. Before Holmes and I could rise from our chairs, he yanked at a lever and the machine shimmered and vanished again, like that same pond reflection when a stone has been thrown into the water. Motes of dust swirled around the floor in the disturbed air and settled before either of us could speak.

"Good heavens, Holmes, did you see?"

"Yes, Watson, I saw. My suspicions are correct."

"Well, what are we going to do now?"

"Now? We are going back to Baker Street. We have an appointment at six with Wiggins."

"But what if he—Willoughby comes back?"

"I expect him to, Watson, and I want him to do so, to finish what he has begun."

"Holmes, I don't understand."

"You will, Watson," said Holmes tucking the journals under his arm, "in time. Now we have some work to do back at Baker Street."

We no sooner had our coats off than Holmes went straight away to the bookshelves and began pulling out one book after another, rifling their pages and dropping them unceremoniously onto the floor. "Come on, Watson, help me."

"Help you do what?"

"If Willoughby has behaved according to pattern, we will find his next prediction in one of these volumes and not have to wait for the benefit of his guidance."

"Oh," I said, and plunged into the task myself.

When Mrs. Hudson knocked at the door Holmes bade her enter, and she and Wiggins were greeted by the sight of three quarters of our library heaped on the carpet. Wiggins stood open mouthed but Mrs. Hudson, long familiar with Holmes's erratic ways said simply, "A gentleman here to see you, Mr. Holmes."

"Thank you, Mrs. Hudson," Holmes said over

his shoulder. "Hello, Wiggins. Have a seat. We'll be with you directly. Better still, come join in."

"We're looking for an envelope hidden in one of these books," I explained.

"Hello!" Holmes exclaimed. "Found you. Shakespeare again; *Julius Caesar* this time." He held up an envelope lettered in the same precise block letters as the others. "This may give us an advantage, Watson." He tore open the envelope and extracted the note.

"Well, what does it say, Holmes?"

"It says that Superintendent Clifton Webb will be murdered at seven o'clock in the excavation tunnels. Come, Watson; you too, Wiggins. We have a head start, but time slips by as we speak." He grabbed his hat and coat from their hooks by the door and before we could move was sprinting down the stairs. "Come on, you two," he shouted up the stairwell.

I looked to Wiggins and shrugged. In no time at all, Holmes had hailed a cab.

"Holmes," I said, "aren't you going to notify Lestrade?"

"Watson, there's no time. I—" he turned his head from side to side and spied a bobby across the street. "Constable!" he called to him. "Tell Inspector Lestrade, 'murder in the tunnel excavation at seven o'clock'." By then, Wiggins and I had piled into the cab. Holmes swung in and shouted, "Go!" to the driver. The perplexed bobby ran after the cab shouting, "Murder? What—?"

"Tell Lestrade Holmes sent you, and hurry," my friend shouted back. We turned a corner, and the bobby fell from sight.

As the cab hurtled through Marylebone, Holmes cast an appraising eye over Wiggins. In a new suit of clothes, clean-shaven and bathed, Wiggins looked a world apart from the creature he had been the day before. "You look adequate, Wiggins," said Holmes. "I judged you correctly."

"Thank you kindly, Mr. Holmes. I suppose I cleans up well. If I may ask, what is it we're about?"

"Knowing the pleasures of Fate."

"Beg pardon, sir?"

"Yes, Holmes, and I must beg your pardon as well," I said with some irritation.

"The passage in *Julius Caesar* where I found the envelope, Act III scene 1, lines 108-110. After the death of Caesar Brutus says to Cassius, 'Fates, we will know your pleasures: that we shall die we know; 'tis but the time and drawing days out, that men stand upon.' If we are quick enough, we shall draw out Webb's days a bit longer. That and pull a foreign thread from the warp and weft. Watson, I hope you still have your pistol."

***

We arrived at the tipple at ten of seven. We found two of Lestrade's men standing guard. They saw us leap from the cab and immediately closed ranks across the portal. As we neared them, I saw that one had a darkening bruise on his jaw. "You can't come in, Mr. Holmes," said one. "No one can; Inspector's orders."

"Moorcock, is it?" Holmes said. The taller of the guards nodded. "Yes, sir." Holmes looked about very convincingly. "Has Inspector Lestrade arrived already? We were to meet him here."

The bobby cocked an eye at Holmes. "No, sir, he ain't. And we have strict orders to keep people out."

"Where is Webb?"

They looked at each other. "In the tunnel, sir." Moorcock's face flushed. "We told him he weren't allowed, and he got a bit belligerent with us. I could smell his breath, and I dare say he was aled up, that one. When we wouldn't budge he kicked my legs from under me and give Ralph here a fist up his jaw and was down the ladder like a bleeding ferret. We'd have gone after him, but we ain't to leave our post."

"It is imperative that we find him at once," Holmes said. "We received this message just moments ago." He handed the latest note to Moorcock who read it and handed it to his partner. "Well, then," Moorcock chuckled, "that saves us the trouble of doing for him later, don't it?"

Holmes face grew hard. "This is no time for levity, man. Someone's life is at stake here. If Webb dies in the next few minutes because you wouldn't let us find him, what will the Inspector have to say about that? He should be here momentarily, but there isn't time to waste. Step aside."

Moorcock and his partner exchanged a glance and moved away from the entrance.

"Come, Watson, Wiggins," said Holmes. "Let us hope we are not too late."

The excavation was eerily still and dim. Only a few of the lamps were lit, leaving shadowed stretches and pockets of darkness along the tunnel. Ahead we heard the distant gurgle of water in a drain and nothing more.

"Where do we look for Webb, Holmes?" I said.

He handed a small lantern to Wiggins and one to me. "Take us to the place where you saw the ghost, Wiggins; use every shortcut you know."

"Aye, Mr. Holmes." Without another word, the little man took off at a brisk pace and we were hard put to keep up with him. Wiggins led us through a crevice here, a passage there, twisting and winding until I don't believe Ariadne's thread would have led us out.

"Not far now, sirs," said Wiggins twisting nimbly through a cleft that wedged me so that Holmes had to grasp my hand and tug me through. I felt the rumble of a train close by.

The cleft opened into a rail tunnel with tracks running as far as we could see. I felt a sense of vertigo as I looked first one way then the other and saw the tunnel's perspective funnel to a pinpoint in either direction. "We'll follow the track now, sirs," said Wiggins. "Mind you, stay away from the third rail. Kill you dead, it will."

"Where are we now, Wiggins," Holmes said, "in relation to the surface?"

"Near to Clapham Junction, sir, just another—"

Wiggins's comment was interrupted by the sound of a gunshot.

He hesitated, listening, then a keening wail echoed down the tube. Wiggins froze. "The ghost," he whispered with almost no voice.

"No ghost, Wiggins, a Morlock. Come quickly." Ahead, I saw a beam of light, and the closer I came to it I realized it was a lantern lying on its side in the rubble beside the tracks.

Holmes led the way into a side tunnel. As I followed, I saw an incredible sight in the beam of his lantern. Webb was on the ground locked in mortal combat with what I thought at first was an albino ape, then I realized except for a shock of flaxen hair from its head to its waist the creature was hairless.

Its arms were unnaturally long, joined to powerfully cruel shoulders and chest. Muscles and tendons bulged like cables through its pale skin as it grappled with Webb for a hand at his throat, but Webb held his own, his arms as long as the Morlock's and his longer legs giving him some advantage. Webb was a brawler and he might have rolled atop the creature but for the narrowness of the tunnel.

In the light of the lanterns, I saw a rivulet of blood coursing down the Morlock's torso. Webb had wounded him with his pistol but nowhere near fatally. Webb's arm broke free and his fist crashed into the creature's jaw. The Morlock rocked back and for a moment I thought Webb had him, but the white beast doubled its fists and delivered a hammer blow to the superintendent's forehead.

Before the monster could finish him off, Holmes, ignoring the hazard, rushed forward and thrust his lantern into the creature's face, shining its beam directly into the monster's pinkish grey eyes.

The Morlock's head snapped back as if yanked by its hair. It gave forth a cry that was half wail and half snarl as it rushed blindly at us and leapt, bowling Wiggins and myself over backward. "After him," shouted Holmes. "Don't let him escape."

The Morlock stumbled into the tube. At the same time, I heard the distant clanking of an approaching train. Its lamp cut through the darkness of the tunnel. "Keep him in sight, Watson," Holmes barked. "Wiggins, see to Webb."

In the bobbing beams of our lanterns we saw the Morlock bounding, hands brushing the floor as if it ran on all fours. Despite its flash blind vision, it moved swiftly and with purpose, perhaps by instinct alone, and I could see that we would lose him in the next side tunnel. Behind us the train came closer, less than a hundred yards and closing quickly.

The Morlock jerked to a halt, shielding its eyes with a bloodied hand and looking across the rails to a shadowy cleft in the tunnel wall.

"Watson, shoot him," said Holmes. "If he crosses the track, the train will cut us off, and we'll lose him."

I raised my revolver to fire. At that instant a beam of dazzling white light fell on the creature's face and it reeled, shrieking and clawing at its eyes. Half blinded myself, I fired, hitting it in the shoulder. The shot spun it round and it fell onto the tracks. The Morlock blindly groped for a handhold to get to its feet and in so doing, grabbed onto the third rail. The current was not sufficient to prove fatal to the creature's odd constitution, but it was enough that it could not let go its hold.

THE AFFAIR OF THE CHRONIC ARGONAUT

The operator frantically rang the warning bell. The train's brakes screeched, but they couldn't stop it before the engine crushed the Morlock under the engine's wheels.

The crew and a number of passengers poured out of the train to peer at the carnage.

"Hurry, Watson," said Holmes tugging at my arm.

"Where are we going now?"

"After the person who blinded our quarry. I expect he's wearing spats and a derby."

We crossed the tracks and plunged into the cleft I'd seen a moment before. It was a cross cut to a drainage channel and after a few hundred feet opened into another rail tube. As we left the passage, we were brought up short by a gunshot and a bullet ricocheting over our heads.

"Come no further, Mr. Holmes." The voice from across the track echoed from one end of the vacant tube to the other.

"Fine gratitude to show the man who's cleaned up your mess, Willoughby."

A chuckle. "You never disappoint, Mr. Holmes. I chose well."

I tried to shine my lantern in the direction of Willoughby's voice and he said, "Don't shine your lamp at me, Doctor, or I'll do for you as I did for the Morlock. My light may not blind you as it did him, but you won't read a newspaper ever again."

"You have an accounting to render, Willoughby," Holmes said. People have died because of what you have done."

"People die every day, Holmes. What of it in the

cause of science?"

"So that puts you above the law and morality? What *hubris*. I asked myself more than once why you have done what you have, and the only answer I find: because you can."

"Don't presume to judge me, Holmes. My motives lie far beyond such pettiness. You have no idea the lengths I've gone to bring us to this point. But you will understand all in due course. Now, however, I must take my leave. Your friend Lestrade will arrive in three minutes with his men and I have no intention of being here when he does. *Adieu.*" After a few echoing footsteps Willoughby was gone.

Precisely three minutes later, we heard footfalls and half a dozen officers with Lestrade in the lead came huffing up the tunnel.

I looked at my watch. "Three minutes exactly, Holmes," I said. "How the devil did he know?"

"Because, Watson," Holmes said *sotto voce*, "our friend has played this scene before, perhaps many times." Then in a louder voice, "Inspector, I see you got my message."

***

We spent the better part of the night sorting it all out with Lestrade. I could see by his manner that he was less than satisfied with our account of events, but as Holmes said, "The crime is solved, Lestrade. The killer is dead, work can resume in the tunnels, and the rich and powerful will stop barking at your heels. All's well that ends well."

"There's got to be more to this," Lestrade snapped. "You can't expect me to believe that creature penned those notes and somehow planted them in your flat."

Holmes shrugged. "Do you believe that he had an accomplice, or that some criminal manipulated the poor demented being into doing his dirty work for him?"

"I don't know, Holmes, but I'd wager you do."

"Even I have my limits, Lestrade, as do we all. The killer is dead. Rejoice in the circumstance. 'Sufficient unto the day is the evil thereof.'"

***

Dawn broke before we returned to Baker Street. Mrs. Hudson caught us on the stairs with a message delivered just after we had departed the night before. Holmes thanked her and slipped it unread into his pocket.

"Aren't you going to read it, Holmes?"

"No need, Watson. I recognize the hand as Willoughby's. I have no doubt that it directs us to *Julius Caesar* act three." We opened the door of the flat to find that all of our books were returned to the shelves.

"Mrs. Hudson has been busy," I said, and then something caught my eye on the table: another envelope.

Holmes snatched it up and stared at it for a moment. His name was written on its face in the same precise letters we had come to recognize as Willoughby's hand. In the envelope were several pages of closely written prose. What follows is a transcription of that text:

16 November 1999

Mr. Holmes,

No doubt, by now you have read Wells's account of my journey into the future and have come to realize that it is based on truth although he presents it as a penny dreadful fiction. I have built the machine he described, one that you have seen, albeit ephemerally, and have travelled back and forth in time more often than you can imagine.

A mind such as yours can appreciate the exasperation I felt at the disbelief my story met among my guests. I realize now that my ego got the better of me. I resolved to prove my account true and returned to 802,701 determined to bring back irrefutable evidence.

As by now you have deduced, I captured a Morlock, one of the underground dwellers of that epoch and brought him back with me to your present. You think John Merrick caused a sensation? Imagine presenting a living Morlock to the Royal Society. I underestimated the cunning of the creature, however; after all, his race was familiar with mechanics, having tended the underground machines for untold centuries. He picked the lock on his cage and escaped.

Then I saw the mistake I had made, not so much because of the deaths he caused, but because of what might result from the proof of my machine and its capability. I realised that the government would not rest until it had the device in its possession and with it do who knows what? And what of the criminal element? What might your old nemesis Moriarty do with such power? No, I cannot let that happen.

I was foolish enough to envision building an even larger machine and gathering the best minds of our time to study the future, a crew of Chronic Argonauts, if you will, but I see now that can never be. Yet to hide so brilliant a light under a bushel was intolerable. I resolved that one person must know, one intellect broad enough to understand and appreciate what I had done, and that would be sufficient. I chose you, Mr. Holmes, and I chose wisely.

I realized that to simply tell you what I have accomplished and even demonstrate the machine for you might not secure your credulity, for your deductive mind is firmly rooted in the material world. I had to orchestrate a mystery, a conundrum sufficiently bizarre as to prove irresistible to you and in so doing bring you to challenge your vision of reality.

Wells told only of my journey into the future and my return to the present, for that was all I had done by that evening. Since then I have travelled into the past as well and learned that events once done can be undone, can be altered, and those who dwell in that stream of time will never know different. What has passed for you as a few days has aged me more than four years, for as I step out of time's natural course, the processes of biology continue unabated.

Once begun, I found I could not stop. So many times I have had to go back and forth to shape events toward a desired end. Set a course into motion, learn its outcome then go back again and alter it.

I have been arrested and detained many times by the police and waited out my sentences. You yourself beat me about the head with your stick. Once, the good Doctor shot me with his pistol as I escaped through the window of your flat. I almost died from the wound. The first time Webb found the Morlock, he shot him dead, which would have upset my plan. I had to slip into the pub where he was drinking, lift his pistol from his coat, and remove one bullet so that his first pull of the trigger would fall on an empty chamber.

But I digress. I knew who would be murdered and after a few jogs back and forth in time, exactly where and when those murders would occur. Gaining access to your flat was simple. It was I who stole Mrs. Hudson's purse. A locksmith copied her keys for me and I returned to her present that afternoon in different garb and gave the urchin the stolen bag. I then could come and go when the house was empty and leisurely browse your library for an appropriate place to hide my messages.

As I have said, you never disappoint, Mr. Holmes. The mystery of the first "prediction" set your mind to work. The second message galvanised you into full deductive mode, and by the third, you had all but solved the case. Imagine my surprise when I returned to my workshop to find you and Doctor Watson sitting in wait. I applaud you, Holmes, not only for your remarkable ability but for your willingness to engage in the teleological suspension of disbelief in pursuit of truth.

THE AFFAIR OF THE CHRONIC ARGONAUT

I have done something at once very great and very terrible and it has taken its toll upon me. I learned too late that layering one reality upon another, so many as I have these past two years, strains the mind in ways I would never have imagined. Holding so many of them indexed in my brain is rather like keeping a warren of rabbits in a box with no lid. I must be watchful lest one of them leap out and if one does, while I pursue the fugitive, others will follow suit.

I end this affair gratified that I have won over the belief of one of the few men capable of truly comprehending and respecting my effort. A few small details require my attention then I will make one last journey. I thought that perhaps I could return to 802,701, to restore humanity and civilization to the world, but I realize that the temptation to come back to this time once again would ever tug at my sleeve. I must go firm in my resolve that I will not return.

I will not alter your current reality, Mr. Holmes for to do so would remove that which allows me to go to my death with a modicum of satisfaction. I want you to remember, perhaps not for all time, but for time enough that my work has not all been a striving after the wind.

Soon—it seems odd to me to speak of time in such terms—I will take my seat in the machine, throw the control lever full force forward, and inject myself with a lethal dose of arsenic. My machine will never stop lest time itself come to an end. It must be done soon while I still control my thoughts.

I thank you, Mr. Holmes for allowing me a brief shining moment of recognition.
Selah,
Robert F. Willoughby

After reading the manuscript, I said to Holmes, "I'm afraid Willoughby has used us rather badly."

"Yes, Watson, like Coleridge's Ancient Mariner, he has burdened us with a tale we must carry to our graves, yet one we cannot tell, for who would listen?" he said, and picked up his violin.

Two days later, I went out on some errands and returned to find Holmes standing at the fireplace. He was feeding sheets of paper into the flames.

"Here, Holmes, what are you burning?"

"Willoughby's journals."

"You read them?"

"Every word. The knowledge they contain is much too dangerous for mortals such as we to guard. Have you seen today's *Times*?"

"Not yet," I replied.

"You will find it on the table open to a story about a fire in Richmond. An abandoned house there burned to the ground."

I picked up the paper and found the article. I quickly read the piece and said, "Yes, that's Willoughby's address."

"He seems to be following his plan to its end."

As I handed the *Times* back to Holmes, a small slip of paper fluttered to the floor. "What's this?"

Holmes snatched it up and studied it for a moment and handed the *Times* back to me. "Watson, turn to the Exchange Report, would you, and look up the status of Pickman Limited."

I ran my finger down the column. "Here it is, Holmes; it sells for just under two pounds per common share."

Holmes drew his watch from his vest and stared at it for a moment as if he had never seen it before. He spread the slip of paper on the table and I recognized Willoughby's careful lettering. It read: Pickman Limited 9 September 1900: £8.2 and below it, "Paid in Full."

***

New Year's Day has come and gone, the false and the true, the cusp of a new century and all of its potential. Mankind looks forward to the dawn of a new age, but I cannot help casting my gaze backward and wondering how much of what I have always known plays false to another reality. Yet as Holmes observed, we mortals are bound to live now, and now. And now.

ABOUT THE AUTHOR

Fred Adams, Jr. is a lifelong Western Pennsylvania resident. He has spent his adult life teaching people to write, and is now retired from the English Department of Penn State University. Since 2014, he has written fifteen books, twelve of them novels in the "New Pulp" genre. He also continues to work as a singer-songwriter, playing solo and with groups in Southwestern Pennsylvania.

He began writing during his undergraduate years at Washington and Jefferson College and sold his first story to a magazine in 1971. Since that time over fifty of his short stories, two non-fiction books, six novels (with six more pending publication as of 2017), and hundreds of feature articles for the Greensburg Tribune-Review have seen print.

He speaks frequently at writer's conferences, and workshops and coordinates the Mount Pleasant Public Library Writers' Circle. His original songs have been recorded onto two CD compilations, The Doctor is In, and Searching for a Vein. In addition, he serves as an associate editor for his publisher, Airship 27 Productions of Denver, Colorado.

How does he describe himself? "I live in abject terror of boredom."

Printed in Great Britain
by Amazon